TORTURE TIME

Skye Fargo figured that when Delgado was a kid, he must have picked wings off flies. Now Delgado was bigger and badder, and Fargo was the one in his hands.

"I could have shot you from ambush as easy as squashing a bug," Delgado said. "But why do that, I asked myself, when I could make you *suffer.*"

"Let me guess," croaked Fargo through cracked lips, straining against the ropes that hogtied him. "You aim to dump me in this desert without food or water."

"You are a smart man." Delago smirked as he took a long pull at his water bag. He let water trickle out of his mouth so Fargo could see it. "And I have another surprise as well. But I don't want to spoil it."

Fargo was willing to wait to find out what that "surprise" was. But he knew he wouldn't be able to. The savage sun was rising fast, and the Trailsman's chances were sinking even faster. . . .

BLAZING NEW TRAILS
WITH SKYE FARGO

THE
TRAILSMAN
123

DESERT
DEATH

by

Jon Sharpe

A SIGNET BOOK

SIGNET
Published by the Penguin Group
Penguin Books USA Inc., 375 Hudson Street,
New York, New York, 10014, U.S.A.
Penguin Books Ltd, 27 Wrights Lane, London W8 5TZ, England
Penguin Books Australia Ltd, Ringwood, Victoria, Australia
Penguin Books Canada Ltd, 10 Alcorn Avenue, Toronto, Ontario M4V 3B2
Penguin Books (N.Z.) Ltd, 182-190 Wairau Road,
Auckland 10, New Zealand

Penguin Books Ltd, Registered Offices:
Harmondsworth, Middlesex, England

First published by Signet, an imprint of New American Library,
a division of Penguin Books USA Inc.

First Printing, March, 1992

10 9 8 7 6 5 4 3 2 1

The first chapter of this book originally appeared in *Gold Fever,*
the one hundred twenty-second volume in this series.

The Trailsman

Beginnings . . . they bend the tree and they mark the man. Skye Fargo was born when he was eighteen. Terror was his midwife, vengeance his first cry. Killing spawned Skye Fargo, ruthless, cold-blooded murder. Out of the acrid smoke of gunpowder still hanging in the air, he rose, cried out a promise never forgotten.

The Trailsman they began to call him all across the West: searcher, scout, hunter, the man who could see where others only looked, his skills for hire but not his soul, the man who lived each day to the fullest, yet trailed each tomorrow. Skye Fargo, the Trailsman, the seeker who could take the wildness of a land and the wanting of a woman and make them his own.

1859, New Mexico Territory,
where the burning sun and the buzzards
claimed as many lives as bullets . . .

1

Skye Fargo was lifting a glass of whiskey to his lips when the first terrified squeal of a horse shattered the tranquillity of a lazy summer afternoon in Albuquerque. He paused, catching sight of himself in the ornately decorated mirror behind the bar. A big man, muscular and hard, he wore the dust of many miles on his buckskins and white hat. His piercing lake-blue eyes narrowed as the frantic whinny was repeated, and he heard other patrons of The Cactus Flower move toward the swinging doors to see what was going on.

The portly barkeep glanced toward the entrance. "What the hell is happening?" he called out. "It sounds like someone is killing that poor horse."

"You're right about that, Charley," responded one of the customers who was gazing out into the wide street. "It's Delgado. He's using his stick on a brown mare."

"Delgado," the barkeep repeated in disgust, and went about wiping the top of the polished bar.

"Who is he?" Fargo inquired.

"Fancies himself a horse trader," Charley answered. "Goes out and rounds up wild horses, then breaks them to sell to the Army or some of the big ranchers hereabouts." He snorted. "Ruins them, is more like it. The bastard beats them every chance he gets. He has a mean streak a mile wide."

"He's not the only one," Fargo said matter-of-factly and downed the whiskey in one gulp. Liquid fire scorched a path down his throat and into his stomach. Pivoting, he set the glass down and headed for the doors, aware of the barkeep's eyes boring into his back. The mare still neighed shrilly, and he could hear loud smacks as the blows were delivered. Someone outside was laughing.

A half-dozen customers were blocking the way out.

9

"Excuse me, gents," Fargo said gruffly.

They turned, took one look, and quickly moved aside so he could pass.

The hot, dry air struck Fargo like a physical blow as he emerged from the saloon. He halted to survey the situation and hooked his thumbs in his gunbelt. To his left and right were pedestrians who had stopped to witness the beating. Most wore Spanish-style attire, as was typical of a town that had been founded by the Spaniards and later controlled by Mexico before the United States acquired the region after defeating her southern neighbor in a two-year war that had ended in 1848. Now, in 1859, there was growing evidence of the increasing American influence in the dress and customs of the people, but Albuquerque retained a distinctly Spanish flavor.

In the center of the street was the focus of attention—four men and a string of horses. One of the men, wearing a black sombrero and black clothes, was furiously beating a small mare with a straight stick carved out of ponderosa pine. As the man swung, he uttered vile oaths, his face flushed red with rage. His three companions, all bearing the grubby, lanky look of inveterate toughs, goaded him on.

The object of Delgado's wrath tried in vain to pull loose, but the horse trader had a firm grip on her plain leather bridle. Blood seeped from five or six wicked cuts, one dangerously close to her eye. She squealed again when her sensitive ear was hit by the stout stick.

Fargo saw disgust reflected in the faces of many of the bystanders, but no one made an effort to intervene. Not that he blamed them. Delgado and his bunch would not take kindly to anyone butting into their affairs, and it wasn't against the law for a man to beat his own horse to death, if the man so chose. But it went against Fargo's grain to stand by and watch an innocent animal, especially a horse, be so harshly mistreated. He'd spent a lifetime around horses, and he'd learned that most horses were as good or bad as the folks who owned them. By and large, horses were dependable, loyal critters, which was more than could be said for quite a few people he'd met in his travels.

"Rear on me, will you?" Delgado roared and planted more blows on the hapless animal's head.

Fargo had seen enough. He strolled into the street, straight toward the man in black. Delgado's men had their backs to him, and none of them realized he was approaching until he stepped forward and seized the stick as Delgado lifted it overhead for yet another swing. With a sharp motion he wrenched the stick from the horse trader's hand and shifted so he faced all four of them.

Delgado, startled, spun. He gawked, as if he couldn't believe his eyes, then blurted, "What the hell do you think you're doing, gringo?"

"You've made your point," Fargo said, the stick in his left hand at his waist, his right hand hovering near his six-gun. He glanced at the other three, who were equally amazed at his audacity.

"You shouldn't poke your nose in where it doesn't belong," Delgado snapped, and nodded at the stick. "Now give that back and go on your way before you make me mad."

In response, Fargo suddenly gripped the stick with both hands and broke it in half over his right knee. He let the two pieces fall to the ground, then straightened. "The mare has been beaten enough," he stated.

Delgado's thin lips twitched as he stared at his broken stick. He hissed like a snake about to strike, his shifty brown eyes darting to the Colt. 44 in Fargo's holster. "Who are you, gringo?"

"The handle is Skye Fargo."

"Do you know who I am?"

"A horse beater."

One of the others, a stocky man with a brown sombrero who wore two guns, tied low, took a half-step forward. "Let's teach this fool a lesson, Delgado."

Fargo never gave them any warning. His right hand flashed up and out, sweeping the Colt in a brutal arc, slamming the barrel into the side of the stocky man's head and dropping him on the spot. The other two grabbed for their hardware, but he covered them with the .44. "Go ahead. Give me an excuse," he said.

Delgado looked at his fallen *compadre,* then at the steady barrel of the big Colt. He licked his lips and said, "You have the upper hand for now, friend. What do you want from us?"

"All I want is the mare left alone," Fargo told them.

"You do this over a stupid horse?" Delgado said, and shook his head in wonder. "You are one crazy gringo."

"So I've been told."

Delgado motioned at his unconscious companion. "Pick up Felipe," he directed the others, "and bring the horses. All except the mare." He grinned at Fargo. "I give her to you, mister."

"I don't want your horse."

"Keep her anyway," Delgado said with exaggerated kindness. "Take good care of her. Tend her cuts. And when I am good and ready, I will come for her." Hatred flared in his eyes. "While you wait for me to come, think about the fact that no one has ever treated José Delgado the way you have and lived long to brag about it." He sauntered off, flipping his hand in a short wave. "Be seeing you around, gringo. You can count on it."

Fargo waited until the quartet and their string of horses took a left turn and were out of sight before he slid the .44 into its holster and turned to the mare. She stood with her head bowed, trembling from her ordeal. "It's okay," he said, patting her neck. "He's not going to hurt you again."

"Maybe not, but I wouldn't bet two cents on how long you'll be among the living."

The friendly voice belonged to a tall man sporting a badge high on the left side of his gray shirt. He wore a black planter's hat and a nickel-plated Colt on his hip. "I'm Clay Bannister," he said, stepping up and offering his hand. "Town marshal."

Fargo shook, noting the lawman's firm grip and unflinching green eyes. "Skye Fargo. Do you make it a habit to let bastards like Delgado beat horses to death in your streets?"

Bannister refused to be riled by the blunt question. "I was five blocks away and got here as soon as I was told about it," he said. "Just in time to hear Delgado threaten you." He pushed his hat back on his head. "And no, I don't let yacks like him do as they please with their animals. If a man gets out of line,

I haul him in for disturbing the peace. Not that it would do much good in Delgado's case. I've warned him about his temper a dozen times, and twice he's spent the night in jail. But he does as he damn well pleases.''

"Too bad his scalp isn't hanging in an Apache wickiup,'' Fargo commented, and stroked the mare to calm her down.

"You'd better watch your back while you're in Albuquerque,'' Bannister advised. "He's not the type to fight fair.''

"Figured as much,'' Fargo said.

"How long will you be here, by the way?''

"Haven't made up my mind yet,'' Fargo told him. "I rode in less than half an hour ago after a week in the saddle.''

"Come in by yourself or with a wagon train?''

"By my lonesome,'' Fargo said, gripping the mare's bridle, amused at how tactful the lawman was trying to be. "All the way from Tucson.''

"Tucson?'' Bannister repeated and whistled in appreciation. "That's a far piece for a lone *hombre* to be traveling.'' He studied Fargo for a moment. "Not many men would risk the heat, the snakes, and the Indians and go it alone. You must be part Indian yourself.''

Fargo saw that the man meant the remark as a compliment. "I reckon you could say that,'' he allowed and looked up and down the street. "Can you recommend a decent livery nearby?''

"There's the Walker stable, about two blocks north and four west.

"Much obliged,'' Fargo said, and walked toward the hitching post in front of the Cactus Flower where he had tied his own horse on arrival. The big Ovaro, a magnificent pinto stallion, bobbed its head and snorted as he came up. "Let's get you some feed,'' he said, and the stallion nuzzled his neck.

"You seem to have a way with horses, Mr. Fargo.''

Fargo turned. The lawman had followed him over. "Do you want something?''

"I'd like to tag along to the livery, if you don't mind,'' Bannister said good-naturedly.

"It's your town,'' Fargo said, and led both horses northward. He sensed that Bannister had something on his mind and figured the man would mention it in his own good time.

"I've been marshal about a year," Bannister disclosed. "Had to bury a few hardcases, but for the most part my job consists of locking up drunks so they can sleep it off and shooting stray dogs when they become a nuisance."

"Must keep you on your toes," Fargo said, and grinned.

"I'm not complaining," Bannister said. "I'd rather be bored to death than get a slug in the back. Albuquerque isn't as wild and raw as some of those new towns like Denver and Kansas City, which suits me just fine. I'm not out to make a reputation for myself by seeing how many liquored-up longhairs I can bury."

Fargo decided he liked the man. Bannister impressed him as being a decent, honest sort, a far cry from the type of lawman who regularly ran roughshod over anyone and everyone.

"Sometimes, though," Bannister went on wistfully, "trouble can't be avoided no matter how hard you try. And then there's hell to pay."

"You must be good at your job or you wouldn't have lasted a year," Fargo commented.

"I do what has to be done," Bannister said, and idly glanced at the saddle on the Ovaro, his gaze lingering on the rifle resting snugly in its scabbard. "I see you carry a Sharps."

"Have for years," Fargo said.

"It's a powerful gun. Not just any galoot can use one. How good are you with it?"

"I usually hit what I aim at."

"Thought so," Bannister said, and scratched his chin. "You might be just the man Mrs. Davenport is looking for."

"Who?"

"Grace Davenport. She's a lady from back East, staying at the Fairmont Hotel on Baker Street. Been here pretty near a month trying to find someone to do some work for her."

"What kind of work?" Fargo asked.

"I'd rather let her tell you," Bannister said. "If I was to do it, you'd swear I'd gone loco."

"I don't like the sound of that," Fargo said.

"At least let me introduce you to her," Bannister said. "She won't be what you expect, believe me. And it might turn out

14

to be well worth your while. She's offering to pay two thousand dollars to the right man.''

Fargo glanced at the lawman. "For that kind of money she should have more takers than she can handle."

"All depends on the job."

"I like it less and less," Fargo said, although his curiosity was aroused. There were men who would do practically anything to have two grand in their pockets, even kill if need be. And although Albuquerque wasn't Denver, there had to be plenty of hard men capable of doing whatever Mrs. Davenport wanted done. Yet no one had taken the job in almost a month. What could it possibly be?

They walked two blocks and turned west, moving down the middle of the street. It was the hottest part of the day, and many of the town's residents were enjoying a siesta or simply sitting in whatever shade was available. Traffic was light.

"How about it?" Bannister asked. "Will you let me introduce you? The Fairmont Hotel isn't far from here, so it won't be much out of your way."

"What's your interest in this?" Fargo queried.

"I just hate to think she'd have to go back to Ohio with a broken heart," Bannister said. "I'd help her myself, but I can't afford to be gone from my job for a month or more."

"A month?" Fargo repeated in surprise and then tensed when he heard the sound of running feet to their rear. He spun, his right hand swooping to his Colt, but he was already too late.

Not fifteen feet away, racing toward them with a shotgun leveled in Fargo's direction, was the man named Felipe, his face a mask of fury.

2

"Felipe!" Bannister barked.

"Don't move, gringo!" the stocky man shouted, stopping and aiming his weapon squarely at Fargo's chest.

Fargo knew there was no arguing with a shotgun under a range of twenty feet. Whoever held one had a distinct advantage in a gunfight. While a pistol or a rifle could be equally deadly, neither spread lead as effectively as a shotgun. And when loaded with buckshot, a shotgun became a small cannon, able to shred flesh with devastating effect. Most hardcases knew this fact, which was why lawmen, bank guards, stagecoach guards, and vigilantes preferred to have shotguns handy in a pinch.

Fargo froze with his hand inches above his Colt, knowing Felipe would blow him in half the instant his fingers touched the butt. He might draw fast enough to get off a shot, but even if he tied Felipe, he was dead. If he did as the man wanted for the moment, Felipe might become careless and give him an opening. He figured Felipe wanted to get in a few words before squeezing the trigger. Why else had he held his fire?

Blood trickled down Felipe's check from the gash in his temple where Fargo's Colt had struck him. He wagged the shotgun barrel and said, "You don't look like such a big man to me now, hombre!"

Fargo said nothing, his eyes glued to Felipe's trigger finger. If it started to tighten he would draw, no matter what the consequences might be.

"Put that shotgun down," Clay Bannister directed.

"Stay out of this, Marshal," Felipe responded without taking his feral eyes off Fargo. "This son of a bitch hit me. I owe him."

"If you kill him like this, it will be murder," Bannister said, taking a few slow steps to the left.

"I don't care," Felipe snapped, now training the shotgun on Fargo's head.

"I'll have to take you in or—" Bannister began calmly.

"You'll try," Felipe interrupted.

"You didn't let me finish," Bannister said. "I'll have to take you in or kill you if you resist. Since you've already told me you're not coming peacefully, I don't have much choice." He lowered his voice. "You can't nail both of us. As soon as you pull that trigger, I'll put a slug in you."

Felipe glanced at the lawman, his forehead creasing in thought.

Fargo still said nothing. A word from him might provoke Felipe into firing. He figured his best bet was to let Bannister handle the situation, but he kept his hand poised just in case.

"What's it going to be?" Bannister demanded. "Either put down that shotgun and live, or make your play and die."

Fargo saw the anger fade from the stocky man's face and allowed his gun hand to relax. The danger had passed.

"Will I have to go to jail?" Felipe asked, lowering the shotgun a few inches.

"No jail time," Bannister said. "You let your anger get the better of you, that's all." He glanced at Fargo. "And some folks, the marshal included, would say you were provoked."

"Do I get to keep my *pistolas*?"

"You know the law. Any man can wear his hardware in town so long as he behaves himself. If he doesn't, he answers to me."

"Very well," Felipe said, his shoulders slumping in resignation, and handed the shotgun to the lawman. "You are a fair man, Marshal. I will do as you want. And I will not cause trouble in your town." He looked at Fargo. "But this isn't over between us, gringo. Not by a long shot." Pivoting, he stalked off.

Expelling a breath in relief, Fargo straightened. "That was close. Much obliged."

"You can pay me back by talking to Mrs. Davenport."

"I forgot all about her," Fargo said, grinning.

Bannister was watching Felipe depart, his mood somber. "One of these days I'll have to deal with Delgado's bunch once and for all," he said, more to himself than to Fargo.

"You handled that real well," Fargo complimented him.

"Felipe is easy to handle. He's a hothead who fancies himself a tough hombre and goes around packing two irons, but he's no hardcase. He made the mistake a while back of falling in with Delgado, who's a born killer, and now he has to prove how mean he can be every time someone looks at him crosswise," Bannister said, and sighed. "I'll regret having to kill him when the time comes."

Fargo resumed heading for the livery. The lawman fell in at his side. Neither said a word until they came to the stable and an elderly man with a cheerful smile stepped out to greet them.

"Howdy, Marshal. What can I do for you?"

"Not a thing, Mr. Walker," Bannister said, and jerked his thumb at Fargo. "But this man needs to put his horses up for a spell."

Walker stepped up to the mare and scowled. "Good Lord! What in the world happened to her?"

"A gent named Delgado," Fargo said.

"That rotten no-account bastard," Walker muttered, tenderly examining the cuts caused by the stick. "He does this all the time. I hope that one of these days a stallion hauls off and kicks his head in. It would serve him right."

"Will you look after her?" Fargo asked.

"Sure thing, mister," Walker said. "I can't abide cruelty to horses. I'll dress the wounds and fix her up proper." He looked at the Ovaro. "And I'll take real good care of your pinto, too. He's a fine animal."

"You know horse flesh," Fargo said. He yanked the Sharps out, then untied his saddlebags and draped them over his left shoulder. "All right, Clay. Show me this Davenport woman."

Walker, about to lead the animals inside the stable, stopped. "Davenport?" he said, and glanced sharply at the lawman. "You're not figuring on hooking this fella up with her, are you?"

"I reckon I am," Bannister responded.

"He must not like you much," Walker said to Fargo. "That woman has been trying to find a man to go chasing windmills for weeks. So far she hasn't had a single taker."

"Windmills?" Fargo asked.

"Yep. You know, like in *Don Quixote*. Don't you read?"

"Not all that much," Fargo admitted.

"Well, *Don Quixote* is all about this pilgrim who puts on a suit of armor and goes around the countryside whacking windmills. He thinks they're giants, you see. And when he's not fighting them, he goes after sheep. Thinks they're enemy armies," Walker related, and sadly shook his head. "The man who agrees to help the Davenport woman will wind up just like in *Don Quixote.*" He made a clucking noise and led the two horses into the livery.

Fargo looked at the lawman. "And you want me to meet her?"

"Pay no attention to him," Bannister said. "Everyone in Albuquerque knows he's a mite touched."

"I wonder."

Bannister indicated the street ahead. "Come on. I'll take you to the hotel."

There were still relatively few people abroad, although Fargo knew that would change in a few hours. During the cool of the evening most folks flocked to the streets for a stroll or rode about in open carriages.

"See any sign of Apaches on your way in?" Bannister inquired.

"A little, but none that was fresh," Fargo said. "They usually stay up in the mountains during the summer months, and I kept to the low valleys."

"Smart man. What about the Navahos? Did you see any sign of them?"

"No. Why? Are they causing trouble again?" Fargo asked. He'd heard rumors that they were. Unlike the Apaches, who lived primarily by hunting and raiding, the Navahos engaged extensively in agriculture. Normally, tribes involved in farming related peacefully to the white man. Not so the Navahos. They continually caused trouble by conducting raids on outlying ranches and waylaying lone travelers and wagons. Far outnumbering the Apaches, the Navahos dominated the region. In recent years they had become bolder in their activities, and there were some politicians who claimed drastic steps would have to be taken to deal with the problem.

"When aren't they causing trouble?" Bannister replied. "The latest attack was a week ago. A rancher living northwest of here had his cattle run off and a worker was killed. The Army sent a patrol after the varmints, but the soldier boys lost the trail."

They came to an intersection and the lawman turned to the right. Midway down the next block reared a white three-story building bearing the stamp of Spanish architecture and a large sign: FAIRMONT HOTEL. Over a dozen buggies and carriages were lined up out front.

The lawman entered first and strolled up to the front desk, where a mousy clerk glanced up and grinned slyly as if at a private joke.

"Well hello again, Marshal. This is a surprise."

"Not near as big a surprise as what will happen if you don't wipe that smirk off your face," Bannister said pleasantly enough, but he leaned over the counter as he spoke and his eyes glinted wickedly.

The desk clerk swallowed hard and was suddenly all business. "What may I do for you, Marshal?"

"Is Mrs. Davenport in her room?"

"No, sir," the clerk answered, and pointed to the right. "The last I saw, she was sitting near the north patio reading the newspaper."

"Thanks," Bannister said, and headed in that direction. He suddenly took off his hat and held it at his side, then ran his hand through his hair. Three times.

Fargo wondered why the lawman should abruptly act so nervous. A few moments later he had his answer, and it had nothing to do with nervousness. They came to a cluster of chairs facing open doors leading to a courtyard. A number of hotel patrons were seated facing the doors. Fargo scanned them, trying to pick out the Davenport woman. Somehow he'd gotten the impression she was middle-aged, a dowager type no doubt, so he was all the more surprised when the lawman stepped up to a chair in which sat a beautiful woman who couldn't be a day over thirty, if that.

"Howdy, ma'am," Bannister said.

Grace Davenport shifted in her seat. She possessed lustrous blond hair and blue eyes that sparkled with vitality. Her full lips were a deep red. The green dress she wore scarcely contained her full figure, and her bosom swelled as she inhaled. "Marshal Bannister. How nice to see you again."

"The feeling is mutual," Bannister said, and motioned at a pair of empty chairs to her left. "Mind if we join you?"

"Not at all," she responded, her gaze darting to Fargo.

Fargo felt as if he were being examined under a microscope. She raked him from head to toe, not missing a thing, then smiled and nodded in satisfaction. Mystified, he sat down, leaned the Sharps against the arm of the chair, and placed the saddlebags and his hat in his lap.

"Who is this gentleman?" Grace Davenport inquired.

"His name is Skye Fargo," Bannister said. "I think he's just the kind of man you've been looking for."

"Do tell."

"Are you still planning to leave in a few days?" Bannister asked.

"I was," she said, "but that depends on whether I'm successful or not." She gave Fargo further probing scrutiny. "If appearances count, I may well be."

"I haven't told him much," Bannister mentioned. "I figured I would leave that up to you."

"Thank you, Marshal," she said, and reached out to place her hand on his. The lawman averted his eyes and coughed. "You have been such a help during my stay in your fair town."

"Only doing my job," Bannister said.

Fargo realized the lawman was enamored of the woman, and he wondered how close the two of them were. He read friendliness in her demeanor, nothing more. Bannister, on the other hand, was as infatuated as a man could be and still retain his presence of mind.

"So why am I here?" Fargo asked. "What is the big secret?"

"There's no secret," Grace Davenport said, facing him. "But if Clay had told you the reason he was bringing you to see me, you probably would have told him to go find someone else."

"I hear you're offering two thousand dollars for whatever you want done," Fargo said.

"True, and the man who takes the job would earn every penny of it the hard way," she replied.

"What does it involve, Mrs. Davenport?"

"Call me Grace," she requested.

Unexpectedly, a beefy man came puffing up to them. He wore a dark suit and a derby and carried a cane, but no gun. "Marshal," he called out loud enough for everyone in the lobby to hear, "you've got to come, pronto."

Bannister frowned. "What is it, Jenks?"

"You're needed at the Acme. Old man Tyler is soused again and threatening to shoot out the chandelier in the gaming room."

Grace Davenport sniffed. "The man is drunk at this time of the day?"

"Tyler never stops drinking," Bannister said testily, and reluctantly stood. "I'm afraid I'll have to go." He put on his hat. "I'm sure the two of you can work things out. If either of you want me, I'll be at the Acme." Hitching at his gunbelt, he hastened off with Jenks on his heels.

"Well, then," Grace said, and got up from her chair to sit down in the one the lawman had vacated, putting her right next to Fargo. "Now we can discuss our business in private." She eyed him yet again. "And I do so hope you're half the man you appear to be."

3

Skye Fargo looked at Grace Davenport, puzzled by the statement. Her tone had implied a double meaning, which couldn't be true. He hardly knew the woman, and it seemed highly unlikely that a prim married woman from back East would extend a veiled proposition minutes after meeting him. Unless, he reasoned, there was more to her than met the eye. He kept his face impassive and said, "Why don't you come straight to the point, ma'am?"

Grace smiled. "You don't believe in beating around the bush. Good. I like that. It shows you're a forceful man unaccustomed to wasting his time."

Fargo made no reply. He let his gaze drift over her bosom again and guessed that she possessed exceptionally large breasts.

"In order to explain why I'm willing to pay such a large sum to the right man," Grace was saying, "I must reveal a bit about my family and my background. I was born and raised in Columbus, Ohio, and I'm the oldest of three children. My mother died when I was ten, and it fell on me to look after my younger sister and brother while my father spent most of his waking hours managing two stores he owned." She paused. "He died two years ago."

Fargo leaned back. He had the feeling she would go on for quite a while. Not that he minded. There were worse pastimes than being in the company of a sensuous, beautiful woman.

"My brother is a captain in the Army, stationed in South Carolina," Grace said. "I sent him a letter and told him what happened. He replied, letting me know he wanted to take care of this matter himself, but the Army won't give him emergency leave. The fools in charge don't believe this qualifies as a legitimate emergency," she concluded bitterly.

"What doesn't?" Fargo inquired.

"I'll get to that in a moment," Grace responded, and went on. "My younger sister is about ten years younger than I am. Two years ago she became involved with the Shakers. Have you heard of them?"

The word jarred Fargo's memory. "They're a religious group, as I recollect, with some mighty peculiar beliefs."

"Many people think so," Grace said. "After my sister became one, I made it my business to delve into the background of the Shakers and find out everything I could about them. I learned they called themselves the United Society of Brethren, and they were started in England about a hundred and fifty years ago. A woman named Ann Lee became their leader, and she was the one who came to America with others in her group."

Fargo suppressed an impulse to yawn. He'd not slept much on the trail and could use a good night's sleep. With an effort he forced himself to stay alert and listen to her tale.

"Everyone calls them the Shakers because during their ceremonies they become very emotional and often quiver and shake as if they have a fit," Grace detailed. "Since coming to America the sect has divided into several factions, and my sister joined one headed by a man named William Shafter."

Please get to the point, Fargo wanted to urge, but didn't. He crossed his legs to keep the circulation flowing and idly brushed dust from his saddlebags.

"Did you know the Shakers don't believe in marriage?"

"So I've heard."

"Not only that, they don't believe in bearing children. The only way they gain new members is by converting them," Grace said, and added, "No wonder there are so few of them."

"Is your sister happy as a Shaker?"

Grace frowned. "She was, the last I spoke with her. You must understand that Gretchen was always a religious girl. She never went anywhere without her Bible. Some might say she was a bit strange because she was never very interested in men, but I know differently. I know her better than anyone else does. She just wanted to serve the Lord in the way she saw fit."

"Nothing wrong with that, I reckon," Fargo commented, at a loss to speculate where the conversation was leading.

"My sentiments exactly," Grace said. "That is, until William

Shafter claimed he could lead his followers to a place where they could live in peace, where they would never again be persecuted for their beliefs or viewed as peculiar, to a veritable Garden of Eden just waiting for them to claim it.''

"Where is this paradise?"

"South of here."

"In Mexico?" Fargo guessed.

"I wish it was," Grace said softly, and elaborated. "Four months ago I received a letter from Gretchen in which she wrote about her intention to follow this Shafter to his Promised Land. I wrote back requesting more details, but she never answered. I was worried so I went to Dayton, where Shafter had a farm that was used as their headquarters. They were gone."

"Every last one?"

"Shafter's sect wasn't very large. The last I knew they only had fourteen members, and eight of them were women. From what I could learn, Shafter sold the farm to buy the wagons and supplies they would need for the first stage of their trek. Then off they went."

"And you haven't heard from your sister since?" Fargo asked, at last able to see where her story was leading.

Grace bowed her head. "No," she said sadly. "From the man who bought the farm I learned that Shafter had said something about heading for Denver, so I went there and asked around all over the town. Eventually I met a store owner who had sold more goods to Shafter, and from him I discovered Shafter's next stop was going to be Albuquerque."

"So you came here."

"Yes. And my worst fears were confirmed."

"How do you mean?" Fargo asked.

"One of the wagons developed a problem with an axle. Shafter brought it in for repairs, and he told the man who fixed it to go over the entire wagon and make certain everything was in working order. When the man asked if Shafter had a long trip ahead of him, Shafter answered that he had about two hundred and fifty miles to travel before he would arrive at his destination," Grace said.

Fargo did some quick mental calculations and suddenly sat bolt upright. "Two hundred and fifty miles south of Albuquerque would be smack dab in the middle of the Jornada del Muerto.''

Grace nodded. ''Exactly. Now you can fully appreciate the reason I'm so worried for my sister's safety.''

Indeed he could. In all Fargo's travels he had never been through the Jornada del Muerto, a remote desert region that was home to the sidewinder, the gila monster, and a few hardy types of lizard, but he'd heard many a tale about the grisly fate of those who'd tried to cross it. Scores of bleached bones were said to mark the spots where hapless souls had keeled over, dead of thirst or hunger, their strength sapped by the blistering sun. Small wonder, then, that attempting to cross the arid expanse of barren wilderness was known as the Journey of the Dead.

''And now it should be obvious why I've been unable to find anyone to go after them,'' Grace went on. ''No one in their right mind goes into the Jornada del Muerto.''

''Maybe the man who repaired the wagon misunderstood,'' Fargo suggested. ''Maybe Shafter took his people another way.''

''I was hoping the same thing until Clay found an old prospector who ran into Shafter's bunch at Adobe Wells,'' Grace said. ''The prospector said he tried to talk Shafter out of going any farther south, but Shafter wouldn't listen.''

Adobe Wells rang a bell. Fargo recollected it was the site of the ruins of an old Spanish mission located a dozen miles north of the Jornada del Muerto, and that a small spring there was the last known source of water between that point and the border with Mexico hundreds of miles to the south.

''So it's a safe bet that Shafter, my sister, and the rest of his sect are now somewhere in the heart of the Jornada del Muerto,'' Grace said forlornly.

''When did this prospector see them at Adobe Wells?'' Fargo asked.

''About five weeks ago.''

Fargo didn't want to say anything, but he doubted very much that the Shakers were still alive. Five weeks was an eternity in the desert, and considering that Shafter and his people were greenhorns who didn't know the first thing about surviving under the extremely harsh conditions existing in that region, it was almost a foregone conclusion that their bones now adorned the arid landscape.

"I know what you're thinking," Grace said, studying his face. "You're like everyone else. You don't believe they're alive."

"The odds are mighty slim," Fargo allowed.

"Maybe so, but I can't just give up and return to Ohio after coming this far. I need to know for a fact whether Gretchen is dead or not," Grace said, inner torment mirrored in her lovely eyes.

Fargo felt sorry for the woman. It was her sister, after all, who had been missing. Since Grace had looked after Gretchen from the time they were small children, it must make the uncertainty over Gretchen's fate almost unbearable.

"Will you help me?" Grace asked bluntly.

Fargo hesitated. He wanted to oblige, but common sense told him he'd be wasting his time, not to mention needlessly risking his life, by venturing into the Jornada del Muerto. The smart thing to do would be to politely decline. "I don't—" he began.

"Is it the money?" Grace interrupted, leaning toward him and placing a hand on his. "I might be able to scrape up some more. But I'm not a rich woman, Mr. Fargo. Two thousand dollars is a lot of money to me. I'm afraid my husband didn't leave me very much when he died."

"It's not the money," Fargo said, his interest aroused by the unfortunate news of her husband. Her palm felt warm on his skin, and his hand tingled as she absently rubbed his knuckles.

"Then what is it? I know you're not afraid. I can tell you're not a coward."

Fargo tried to let her down easy. "It's just that I wouldn't want to take your money for nothing."

"In other words, you don't expect to find them alive."

"No, ma'am, I truly do not," Fargo admitted, and felt her fingers dig into his flesh.

"Gretchen is alive, I tell you!" Grace declared. "Don't ask me how I know, but I do know beyond a shadow of a doubt that she isn't dead. If I could, I'd go after her myself, but everyone says I wouldn't last two days in the desert, and I believe them." She paused, moisture forming at the corners of her eyes. "Please."

Fargo opened his mouth to decline, but the desperate look on her face and the silent, pitiable appeal in her gaze stopped the words from forming. How could he decline, knowing she would be in misery for the rest of her years? Knowing she would carry the burden of uncertainty to her grave?

"I'm begging you."

"Don't," Fargo said, and sighed. "There's no need."

Grace instantly brightened. "You'll go?"

Feeling as if he were the biggest dunderhead in the Territory, Fargo slowly nodded. "I'll try to find your sister for you," he said. Suddenly Grace was out of her chair and giving him a firm hug, her chest mashing against his own, her smooth cheek touching his, her fluttering breath fanning his ear. He automatically responded, looping an arm around her slender shoulders, and felt his pulse quicken.

After a minute Grace stepped back, smiling broadly, tears of happiness streaking her cheeks. "Thank you, Mr. Fargo," she said softly, and dabbed at her eyes with her sleeve.

"Just call me Skye."

"This means more to me than you will ever know," Grace said. "I'll never be able to fully express my gratitude."

"Save your thanks until I get back," Fargo advised. He added silently: If I get back.

"When will you start?"

"Tomorrow morning, I reckon. I need some sleep, and I'll need to buy a pack horse and supplies. Jerky, water bags, and other essentials."

"All expenses will come out of my pocket, naturally," Grace assured him. "Whatever you require, get."

"Don't worry on that score," Fargo said. "A man who goes into the desert without the proper gear is a fool. All the things I'll need will set you back a pretty penny."

"How much?"

"Between two and three hundred dollars," Fargo estimated.

"I thought it might be even more," Grace said, and motioned toward a flight of stairs leading up to the second floor. "If you'll be so kind as to escort me to my room, I'll get the money for you."

Standing, Fargo donned his hat, slung the saddlebags over

his left shoulder, and picked up the Sharps with his left hand. "Lead the way," he said.

Grace hastened toward the stairs. "I have a photograph of Gretchen taken about three years ago that may prove helpful. You're welcome to take it, if you like."

"That won't be necessary. The less I pack along, the better," Fargo said. "I would like to see it, though." He trailed her upward, admiring the manner in which her hips swayed as she walked.

They turned to the right at the landing and went to the last door at the end of the hall.

"This is mine," Grace said, producing a key. She unlocked the door and indicated he should enter first.

"After you," Fargo said, and walked in on her heels to find himself in a comfortably furnished sitting room. Through an open door on his left a large bed was visible.

"Why not make yourself comfortable?" Grace proposed, stepping around him to shut the door, her shoulder brushing his.

Fargo moved to a cherry-red sofa, leaned his rifle against the arm, and deposited the saddlebags on the cushion. He pivoted, about to sit down, when to his surprise Grace Davenport came boldly up to him and impulsively planted a kiss full on his lips.

4

Not one to let a golden opportunity pass, and already stimulated by her mere presence, Fargo responded to the kiss, his tongue flicking out to touch the tip of her own. The sweet taste of her caused a stirring in his loins, and he lightly ran his hands up and down her spine. She arched her back, her body flush with his.

At last she drew back and grinned self-consciously. "Oh, my. That was nice. It has been a while since a man held me."

"What did I do to deserve it?" Fargo asked, puzzled by her motive. She didn't strike him as being a loose woman. Not that he had anything against loose women. Some of them were his best friends.

Grace shrugged. "It was just another way for me to say thank you."

"Say it again," Fargo prompted, and was delighted when she obediently melted into his arms. Their lips met once more, and he could feel the heat her body generated through his clothes. His manhood surged to attention, his heart beat faster.

Their kiss lingered on and on. Grace broke it at last and pressed her palms to his broad chest, her cheeks acquiring a crimson tinge as she averted her eyes. "What have I done?" she said to herself. "You must think I'm a hussy."

"Not at all," Fargo said, and pecked her on the cheek. She shivered as if cold, then cooed.

"Mmmm. You have no idea how this makes me feel."

"You can feel even better," Fargo said, and attached his lips to her left earlobe. She squirmed, inciting him to trace a path of soft kisses around her neck to the bottom of her throat. His hands were on her shoulder blades, and he suddenly brought them both in front to cup her huge breasts.

"Ahhhh," Grace said, gripping his shoulders and burying her face against his neck.

Fargo knew she had told the truth. Judging by her reactions, it had been a long time since she'd shared her body with a man. She gave the impression of being starved for intimate companionship, and he was just the hombre to oblige her. He massaged her breasts and felt her hot tongue lick his skin.

"Oh, yes," she breathed.

Kissing her on the mouth, Fargo let his right hand slide down over her flat abdomen to the mound at the junction of her thighs. She trembled violently and clung to him as if drowning in her passion. He rubbed his palm in small circles until she gasped, then abruptly scooped her into his arms and walked into the bedroom.

Grace had her eyes closed. She breathed heavily, her bosom straining against her dress.

Tenderly, Fargo placed her in the middle of the bed, then hastily removed his boots, gunbelt, and hat. She still had her eyes closed when he aligned himself beside her. Leaning down, he nibbled on her lips and chin. His right hand swept to her breasts, causing her to moan.

Fargo was in no mood to hurry. He was hungry for some affection himself, and he intended to savor her as if she were a rare delicacy. Again they kissed, their tongues entwining, and he began to unbutton the front of her dress, working from the top down. It took a while, but eventually he exposed both of her breasts, and the sight took his breath away.

Grace was endowed with exquisite globes peaked by pink nipples now hard with desire.

He glued his mouth to her right breast, his tongue flicking the nipple, and felt her fingers in his hair. His hand tended to her other nipple, and in short order she was thrusting herself into him and panting.

"Yes, Skye! That feels so nice! Yes! Yes!"

Fargo dallied at her mountains, licking and sucking and massaging until they were infernos. Slowly, so as to heighten her anticipation, he lowered his right hand across her stomach to her thighs. He gripped the material and hoisted the hem

31

upward until her silken legs were fully revealed, and gently stroked them, deliberately refraining from touching her womanhood.

"Oh! Oh!" Grace gasped.

He entwined his fingers in her nether hair, then slipped a finger between her legs. She was hot and moist and ready as could be. Yet he held off still, stoking her inner fire by caressing her, but not penetrating her inner recesses.

"Please!" Grace cried. "I want you. I want you now."

Fargo accommodated by inserting a finger into her womanhood. She clamped her legs on his arm and sank her fingernails into his back, breathing loudly. His lust rising, he started sliding his finger back and forth, in and almost out, over and over and over. Her hips came off the bed as she ground her mound into his hand, and his fingers became slick with her juices.

"Uhhhh! Uhhhh!" Grace panted.

He persisted for minutes on end, until her entire body throbbed and his own reciprocated, until his organ pulsed with its need. Then he stripped off his pants, knelt between her legs, touched the tip of his manhood to her slit, and, when her erotically hooded eyes met his, rammed into her to the hilt.

"Eeeee! Oh, God!" Grace cried, and clasped him close. "I want you! I want you! I want you!"

Fargo rocked on his knees, pumping his hard organ deep into her core. Her legs came up, hooking over his shoulders, giving him a better angle of penetration. Her hunger was insatiable now, and she melded her body to his, her lips locked on his mouth, her hands roving ceaselessly over his body. The intensity of his thrusts increased, the tempo of his rhythm heightened, and he felt the explosion building at the base of his manhood.

"Now!" Grace wailed. "Please! Now!"

"Now," Fargo growled, and let himself go, filling her to overflowing. She thrashed and gasped and clung to him, cresting in a tidal wave of sexual ecstasy, her belly slapping against his, her large breasts bouncing wildly. It seemed as if he pumped forever, and then his manhood was spent and he gradually coasted to a stop, collapsing on top of her, wet with sweat from head to foot. She went limp under him, her hands draped on his shoulders.

"Oh, goodness," Grace whispered in awe. "I never knew it could be this way."

Fargo rolled onto his side and gazed into her eyes. "Now, that was what I call a proper 'thank you.' "

Grace laughed. "I'll tell you a little secret," she said.

"What?"

"I might have brought you up here even if you'd said no. From the moment I laid eyes on you, I wanted you," Grace said, and added thoughtfully, "I haven't felt this way about a man in ages."

"Lucky me," Fargo said, and kissed her neck.

"My poor Thomas would roll over in his grave if he knew," Grace said. "He's been dead three years now, you see. Went off fishing with a few of his friends and came back with the worst cough you ever heard. The doctor diagnosed it as pneumonia. Tom died a month and a half later."

Fargo said nothing. What could he say? He hadn't known the man, and false sentiment wouldn't soothe her sorrow.

"I never did like for him to go off and leave me for weeks at a time and just to catch a bunch of stupid fish," Grace said bitterly. "If I ever marry again, I'll break every fishing pole the man owns."

"Clay Bannister wouldn't mind," Fargo mentioned.

"Clay is sweet, and I know he's interested in me, but the feeling isn't mutual," Grace responded. "I like him as a friend, that's all."

"Stick around a while and he might make you change your mind," Fargo predicted.

Grace shifted to give him a quizzical stare. "And what about you? Do you go fishing a lot?"

"No," Fargo said. "But I'm not ready to be roped yet, either. It'll be a spell before a woman puts her brand on me, if ever."

"Oh," Grace said, and frowned. "I didn't realize. Thanks for being honest with me."

Fargo knew he'd inadvertently hurt her feelings, but he'd rather be brutally frank than have her get her hopes up only to have them dashed later. "Don't take it personal," he said.

"No. Of course not," Grace replied, her tone belying her words.

He propped himself on an elbow and tenderly stroked her silken blonde hair. "A man knows when he's ready for a hearth and home, and until that time there isn't a thing in the world any woman can do to hogtie him. The harder a woman tries, the more skittish the man becomes. That doesn't mean the man can't like a woman, can't care for her a lot. It just means the man isn't ready."

Grace pondered his statement for a minute, then gave him a peck on the tip of the chin. "I understand. Thank you again. There are no hard feelings, I promise you."

"Good," Fargo said. "Now, what do you say to the two of us getting a little sleep? Then I'm going to see about buying the things I'll need if I hope to get in and out of the Jornada del Muerto alive."

She put her arm around his neck and kissed him, then said, "Don't talk like that. You'll make it back. You have to."

Fargo lowered his head to one of the pillows and closed his eyes. "Don't fret yourself on my account. I aim to come back, believe me."

"I would never forgive myself if something happens to you."

"Drop the subject and get some shut-eye."

Grace gently touched his cheek. "I mean it, Skye. If you truly think the journey is so dangerous that you won't survive, don't go."

Cracking his right eyelid, Fargo saw her earnest, sincere expression and mustered a reassuring smile. "I'll make it back," he reiterated. "I've been in deserts before, and I know the tricks a man needs to know to get by. Most of my life has been spent in the wild. I'm not bragging when I say I have a better chance of finding your sister than anyone else in Albuquerque."

"Just so you take real good care of yourself."

"You can count on that."

Three hours later Fargo was awakened by something jabbing him in the ribs. He opened his eyes to find that Grace had accidentally poked him with her elbow in her sleep. Grinning, he eased off the bed, straightened, and stretched. His mind felt sluggish, his muscles a bit sore. He could use another eight hours in the sack, but he wanted to obtain the gear he'd require before nightfall so he could leave at first light the next day. He dressed quietly and was strapping the Colt around his waist when he heard a rustling noise from the bed.

"Off after the supplies?" Grace asked.

"Yep. I'll be needing that money now."

Grace rose, modestly turning to button her dress, and then moved to a large oak dresser in the corner. Opening the top drawer, she removed a handbag and took out a small wad of bills. "Here," she said, peeling off three hundred dollars. "This should suffice. If you need more, just tell me."

"Will do." Fargo took the money and stuffed it into his pocket. "Be back in an hour or two."

A seductive smile curled her rosy lips. "Good. It will give me time to wash up."

He touched the brim of his hat, then departed, barely paying attention to the people he passed as he went downstairs and out into the street, preoccupied with making a mental list of the items he would need. The livery stable was his first stop, where he found Walker feeding hay to the mare. "Howdy," Fargo greeted him.

"Well, if it isn't Don Quixote," Walker said, and chuckled. "Did you meet the Davenport woman yet?"

"Sure did."

Walker stopped slinging the hay and leaned his pitchfork against the stall. "I know it's none of my business, but I'm a nosy cuss. Are you going?"

"I told her I'd take the job."

The stable owner cackled and slapped his thigh. "Well, it takes all kinds. And here I pegged you for a sensible man."

"I'll need a pack horse," Fargo said.

Walker snorted. "A horse, hell. You'll need more luck than any man has a right to expect and eyes in the back of your head at all times." He shook his head. "You're not a greenhorn, so for the life of me I can't understand why you're willing to go off and commit suicide."

"The pack horse," Fargo reminded him.

"Touchy hombre, aren't you?" Walker responded. "All right. Let's see now." He walked down the center aisle, regarding the horses on both sides, and thoughtfully stroked his chin. "I've got three or four here you can take your pick from. How much are you willing to spend?"

"If you have a good animal, I'll meet your price," Fargo replied.

"Hmmmm," Walker said, and halted in front of a stall containing a fine, big roan. "This one has carried packs before, and it's as strong as they come. It'll carry anything you care to take."

"It's too damn big," Fargo said. "A horse that size guzzles water by the gallon. I need a smaller animal, one suited to desert travel."

"Oh, that's right," Walker said. "Sorry, pardner. I wasn't thinking there." He walked farther and stopped beside another stall, occupied by a small bay. "How about this critter? It's lean, tough, and won't need to drink near as much as the roan."

Fargo stepped to the stall and critically examined the animal. He liked what he saw. "This one will do. How much?"

"For you, a hundred and thirty dollars. And I'm cutting the price because I like you."

"I'd hate to hear what you charge folks you don't like," Fargo said, and nodded at the bay. "Ninety dollars is as high as I'll go."

"Ninety?" Walker sputtered. "Why, that's robbery, plain and simple. I thought you said you'd meet my price."

"I didn't count on you being such a fourflusher," Fargo said. "Ninety dollars. Take it or leave it."

"A fine bay like this? It's worth a hundred if it's worth a penny."

"Suit yourself," Fargo said with a shrug. "This isn't the only livery in town." He started to turn.

"Now hold on," Walker said. "Don't go off in a huff. Let's negotiate."

"Ninety dollars," Fargo said.

"Ninety-eight."

"Ninety."

"Ninety-five."

Fargo placed his hands on his hips. "I don't have all day for this. Ninety dollars, mister. Take it or leave it."

The stable owner adopted a hurt expression. "It's a sad state of affairs when people take advantage of a man's kind nature. Everyone in Albuquerque knows I'm generous to a fault." He sighed and made a gesture of resignation. "If you want to be a hardcase, then so be it. I'd hate to see you go into the desert with an inferior animal, so out of the goodness of my heart I'll let you have this here bay for ninety-one dollars."

Exasperated, Fargo glanced at the horse. He wasn't about to stand around haggling, nor did he want to waste time going to another livery if he could purchase a pack horse right then and there. Ninety-one dollars wasn't a bad price, all things considered. "All right. You've got a deal."

Walker snickered and rubbed his hands together. "I did it again," he said gleefully.

"Did what?"

"I would have let the bay go for eighty."

5

Fargo was ready to leave at the crack of dawn. Grace came with him to the livery to see him off and silently stood watching him strap his supplies to the pack horse and saddle the Ovaro. When he swung up, she stepped forward and offered her hand.

"Please take care of yourself."

"Will do," Fargo said, taking his fingers in his and giving them a gentle squeeze. He glanced to one side, where Walker leaned against a stall, and nodded. "Adios."

"Watch your back, Don Quixote."

Putting his spurs to the Ovaro, Fargo rode out of the stable and down the street. He turned to the south at the first junction and looked back at the livery just before other buildings blocked it from his view. Grace Davenport still stood there, her arms clasped at her waist, the picture of frail despondency, as if she regretted her decision or was afraid she'd never set eyes on him again. A moment later she was lost to view, and Fargo concentrated on the matter at hand.

There were few citizens abroad at such an early hour, and Fargo reached the southern edge of the town just as the sun rose above the eastern horizon. The air was still cool, but he knew it wouldn't be for very long. He patted the full water bag slung over his saddle horn and then glanced at the three extra bags hanging on the pack animal. They should suffice until Adobe Wells, and once there he would refill them for the trek into the Jornada del Muerto.

He followed the road southward, a dusty track that would eventually take him to Socorro if he stayed on it. But he intended to cut into the wilderness long before Socorro.

He passed travelers heading into Albuquerque: *vaqueros* in their sombreros, close-fitting leather chaparajos, and huge Spanish-style spurs; farmers in the traditional white garb of peons; and occasionally an elaborate carriage carrying a wealthy rancher or his family. The vaqueros invariably nodded in greeting, the farmers offered cheery hellos in Spanish, and the drivers of the carriages gave him a wide berth.

The temperature steadily climbed, the heat becoming intense by noon. He tried not to dwell on how much hotter it would be in the desert. From past experience he knew to keep his motions to a minimum, his hat low over his brow, and his red bandanna loose around his neck. He sweated profusely, which was good. The moisture cooled his skin and made the heat tolerable.

A sparse stand of trees at the side of the road served as his shelter for a midday stop. He took a handful of jerked beef from one of his packs, grabbed a water bag, and sat in the shade, grateful for the respite. Waves of heat rose from the nearby road, reminding him of what lay in store, and he hoped he hadn't bit off more than he could chew.

Marginally refreshed, he resumed his journey. The afternoon dragged by. He held the Ovaro to a walk. Anything faster would unnecessarily sap the stallion's strength, and it would need to be in top form once they arrived at the desert.

When at last evening descended and faint puffs of cool air fanned his face, he smiled in satisfaction. He camped at the base of a grassy knoll situated near a wash through which a trickle of water flowed. Both animals drank greedily and he let them have their fill, then bedded down for the night. For the longest time he lay on his back with his head propped in his hands and marveled at the celestial spectacle overhead. Whether because of the dry, clear air or the time of the year, there were an exceptional number of stars, a multitude of sparkling dots filling the heavens from one end to the other.

Twice he heard coyotes yipping in the distance, and once an owl voiced its eternal question much closer. Neither sound bothered him. He was accustomed to animal noises, to the natural rhythms of the frontier. Where others might stay awake listening anxiously and jumping at every little noise, he slept as soundly as a bear in hibernation and woke up raring to go.

His enthusiasm waned by noon. The heat penetrated into every pore of his skin, and beads of sweat dripped from his chin. He was always thirsty, but he deliberately rationed his water and gave sparingly to the horses, though allowing them proportionately more than he took. By afternoon he reached a point to the northwest of the Los Pinos Mountains, and he left the road behind to ride in the southeastern direction.

The range was aptly named, a rolling series of piñon-covered mountains that stretched to the northern edge of the Jornada del Muerto. Toward nightfall he came on a stream, actually little more than a line of interconnected shallow pools, and bedded down. More coyotes serenaded him than the night before, which didn't stop him from readily dozing off.

Morning found him in the saddle and bearing due south. The piñon became scarcer and scrubbier, the soil harder and drier. Because he wasn't pushing the horses, he didn't come within sight of the Jornada del Muerto until late in the afternoon. He reined up on the crest of the last, low mountain and spied the edge of the desert approximately fifteen miles away.

There was no mistaking where the desert began. The land was flat for as far as the eye could see except for occasional mesas rearing their sheer, bleak rock walls high into the sky. There were sparse pockets of vegetation, no more than green dots from such a distance, either cactus, creosote bush, mesquite, or white and purple sage. That would change, he knew, the farther south he went. Some parts of the desert were totally barren.

Much closer, not more than three miles off, stood the stark ruin of Adobe Wells. The jagged silhouette of a mission wall bore eloquent witness to the religious zeal and determination of the early Spaniards. They had penetrated into the most remote corners of the territory in their quest to convert the natives, often at the point of a conquistador's sword.

He slowly descended the mountain and made for the ruins. The day before he'd left Albuquerque, as he'd gone about buying supplies, he'd asked about the spring and learned it was located less than thirty yards due east of the old mission, at the base of an immense boulder.

When still a mile off, Fargo drew the Sharps and inserted a round into the chamber. The spring had been there for ages. Its existence was common knowledge, not only among the

Americans and the Mexicans but also among the Apaches and other tribes. Indians crossing the region would be bound to stop there, so he must stay alert until he confirmed whether any were present.

There were no horse tracks anywhere, shod or otherwise, which encouraged him. Had a war party visited the spring recently, there would be sign. Half a mile from his destination he abruptly reined up. Imprinted deeply in the sandy soil was the distinct impression of a wagon wheel, and he surmised that one of Shafter's wagons had made it. There were no others, however, indicating the wagon had hit the soft spot and kept on going without difficulty.

He drew within a hundred yards of the mission and halted in a gully. Dropping down, he ground-hitched both animals, then crept forward until he clearly saw the ruins. Only two walls still stood, the one he'd seen from afar and a shorter one opposite. The other mission walls were now rubble, as was most of the perimeter wall that once afforded protection from hostiles.

Nothing stirred.

Staying bent at the waist, Fargo advanced until he was beside the remains of the outer wall. He scanned the interior, saw no reason to be alarmed, and jumped over the collapsed adobe. Sprinting to the high wall, he crouched at its base and scoured the immediate vicinity. Other than a small lizard that darted into the brush, he was the only living thing at Adobe Wells.

Still not satisfied, he left the shelter of the wall and jogged the required distance due east. The boulder, as big as a frame house, was impossible to miss, and the oval pool at the bottom was a welcome sight. He examined the ground around it and found no human footprints. Nor, for that matter, were there any animal tracks, which puzzled him. There was plenty of small game in the area, and unless the animals knew of another water supply they would visit the spring daily.

He shrugged and knelt. There must be a logical reason for the absence of tracks, and he would think about it later. Right at the moment all he wanted was to quench his thirst. He placed the rifle down at his side, leaned forward, and cupped his hands in the cool liquid. A sample taste showed the water to be slightly metallic, but he didn't mind. Desert travelers couldn't afford to be choosy about the water they drank.

Several mouthfuls refreshed him greatly. He picked up the Sharps, hastened to the gully, and retrieved his animals, promptly leading them to the spring so they could satisfy their own craving. As they gulped, he gazed southward. Tomorrow he would enter the desert. There should be enough wagon tracks to guide him on his way, even though the trail was weeks old. Unlike horse and human prints, which could be covered in minutes by blowing dirt or washed away by a single brief rain, wagon ruts could last months before eradication by the elements.

He held the Sharps in the crook of his right arm and scanned the ground around the spring again. Something about it bothered him, nagged at the back of his mind, but he couldn't figure out what. He surveyed the landscape in all directions but saw nothing to explain his uneasy feeling. Still, he'd learned to rely on his instincts, so when he led the horses back toward the mission he was doubly alert.

Since camping beside the spring invited trouble from roving Indians who might stop for a drink, Fargo decided to unroll his blanket at the base of the high wall. He unsaddled the Ovaro, removed the packs from the bay, and settled down for another quiet night. To minimize the risk of being spotted from afar, he kept his fire very small.

As he sat beside the crackling red and orange flames, munching on a tangy piece of jerky, a faint sound wafted out of the descending darkness, coming from the Jornada del Muerto, the indistinct report of a distant shot. Surprised, Fargo faced southward and listened intently. Minutes went by and there wasn't another one. He wondered if his ears had played a trick on him.

Leaning his back against the wall, he watched the sky become inky, the stars blossom. He finished his jerky and went to lie down, then froze when the Ovaro suddenly lifted its head and looked to the northeast, its ears pricked. A second later the big stallion snorted and pounded a front hoof on the ground.

Fargo was instantly upright, the Sharps clutched firmly. The Ovaro knew something was out there, and it had to be something larger than a rabbit or a polecat because the stallion never became agitated over small animals. He had to investigate.

Cautiously, moving in a crouch, he glided along the wall until he came to the end. He left the fire burning. If there was someone lurking in the dark, whoever it was might become suspicious should the flames be abruptly extinguished. He flattened and probed every bush and deep shadow. Not so much as a leaf fluttered.

Fargo crawled out into the open, snaking along silently, until he came to some sage. He knelt, cocking his head, his ears straining, and tensed when he heard a distinct but stealthy footfall. Indians, he reasoned, and went prone again. No one else would be skulking about the ruins at night.

He guessed it must be Apaches. If so, they'd try their damnedest to take his hair. It was a safe bet there was more than one because Apaches rarely traveled alone at night. His best hope was to kill a few, and maybe the rest would leave.

Fargo resumed crawling, angling toward brush a dozen yards to his left. Once there he lay still and waited. Sooner or later one of the warriors would give himself away. He carefully cocked the Sharps, holding the stock close to his chest so his body would muffle the click of the hammer.

To the east a coyote wailed and was promptly answered by another to the northwest.

Fargo wondered if the Indians had just arrived or if they had been at Adobe Wells a while. He thought of the soil around the spring, and insight dawned. There had indeed been a reason he couldn't find any tracks. The Apaches probably had arrived well before him, then had used branches to obliterate every vestige of their visit, wiping the soil clean and removing all animal tracks in the process.

From his rear came a soft thud.

Fargo shifted and looked toward the high wall. His fire was barely visible, and he could just distinguish the outlines of the horses. He debated whether to sneak back and lead them away from the ruins, concerned the Apaches might try to steal them. His mind was made up the next moment when the Ovaro whinnied.

He knew the stallion's voice well, knew the tones the pinto used to express hunger, impatience, fear, and rage. Just now the Ovaro was upset by something—or someone—close by, and it didn't take a genius to figure out what the cause might be. Twisting around, Fargo quickly crawled to the wall, not as attentive now to the noise he made because of his worry over the horses.

He crouched in the blackest shadow, then edged forward until he saw both horses were gazing westward at a thicket bordering the rubble of the outer wall. If there were Apaches watching his camp, they would see him grab the animals. But it couldn't be helped. A man afoot in such rugged country stood a slim chance of survival. He must get the horses to safety.

Fargo touched his finger to the trigger, ready to fire, as he hastened over to the Ovaro. There were no savage yells, no shots or whizzing arrows. He gripped the reins with his left hand and went to the bay, which bobbed its head skittishly. Taking its reins in his hand as well, he headed to the south, staying low, his eyes darting right and left.

Thankfully, he reached the outer wall unchallenged. A gap in the middle enabled him to lead the horses into a stand of piñon, where he tied the reins to a branch. Perplexed because the Indians had yet to make their presence known, he walked to the edge of the stand and studied the mission grounds. Out of the corner of his right eye he detected swift motion and whirled toward it, trying to level the Sharps. There was a swishing sound, and a hard object crashed into the side of his skull. Brilliant dots of light exploded before his eyes, and his legs buckled. He felt his knees strike the ground. Stunned, he tried to pinpoint his assailant, to get off a shot, but all he saw was a vague shape that sprang into view at the very instant another blow to his head plunged his consciousness into a bottomless black pit.

6

"The big bastard is coming around."

"Good. I want him to know we were the ones."

Fargo heard the statements a heartbeat before excruciating pain racked his head. The words were distorted, as if the speakers were at the far end of a long tunnel. Someone groaned, and he realized it was himself. He became aware of a rocking motion, of being on his stomach on something that was moving, then inhaled the pungent, unmistakable scent of horse sweat.

"I can't wait to see the gringo's face," a gruff voice said.

Fargo thought he should know that voice, but his sluggish mind, tormented by pain, was incapable of identifying the person. Belatedly, he realized his wrists were bound and the rope was cutting into his flesh. He opened his eyes and immediately wished he hadn't as the bright sunlight sent shafts of fire stabbing into them.

"We meet again, *bastardo*, eh?"

Blinking, Fargo focused on a large shape near his head, a shape that materialized into the black-garbed Delgado astride a brown stallion. "You," he said, the word croaking from his dry throat.

"The last person you ever expected to see," Delgado said, and laughed wickedly, triumphantly.

Another rider came up alongside Delgado. "Remember me, gringo?" asked Felipe.

Fargo didn't bother to answer. He looked down at the hide of the horse he was on and recognized the Ovaro's black and white coloring. The pinto was being led by another of Delgado's men. Glancing behind the Ovaro, he saw the fourth hardcase leading the bay he'd purchased in Albuquerque.

"Would you like to know how we knew you would be at Adobe Wells?" Delgado asked.

"No," Fargo said, his chin sagging against the Ovaro. He wasn't about to give the son of a bitch the satisfaction of gloating over his capture.

"I'll tell you anyway, gringo," Delgado said, and chuckled. "We were drinking at a saloon when we heard the news. For a month now everyone in town has been talking about that crazy woman, Davenport, who wanted to hire someone to go into the Jornada del Muerto after her loco sister. So when it was learned that you had decided to take the job, the word spread fast." He paused and slapped his thigh, grinning happily. "At first I was glad. I figured you'd go into the desert and die. But then I got to thinking that a tough hombre like you might make it back, after all. So I figured I'd make sure you didn't."

Fargo closed his eyes. He didn't want to hear the rest, but he had no choice. Beads of sweat lined his brow, and his back was uncomfortably hot. The burning sun on the top of his head told him his hat was gone.

"Everyone knows that anyone going into the Jornada del Muerto stops at Adobe Wells on the way," Delgado was saying. "When we were at the saloon, we heard tell you had been going all over town buying supplies. I knew you would leave the next day. And that is when I had my inspiration."

"Don't you ever shut up?" Fargo snapped.

Delgado clucked a few times. "I didn't reckon on you being such a poor loser." He snorted sarcastically. "I knew if we left Albuquerque that night, we'd easily beat you to Adobe Wells. So we each filled a water bag and off we went." He grinned and mopped his sleeve across his sweaty forehead. "We had to ride like hell and nearly killed our horses, but it was worth it. We got there a full day before you did, which gave us plenty of time to erase our tracks and set our little trap. Pretty clever, no?"

"No," Fargo said, deliberately baiting him.

"I know better," Delgado said. He squared his shoulders and glared at Fargo. "And now you know why no one dares prod José Delgado. I will go to any lengths to get revenge on those stupid enough to insult me."

Fargo had to admit that he never would have expected the

man to pull such a stunt, but he wasn't about to say so to his captor.

"Actually," Delgado continued, "I had it in my head to shoot you on sight. We didn't know the route you would take, so we couldn't very well ambush you along the trail, or I might have done that. Adobe Wells was the place to kill you. But on the way there I gave the matter a lot of thought. Shooting you from ambush would have been as simple as squashing a bug, no? But why do that, I asked myself, when we could make you *suffer*?"

Now Fargo knew the reason he was still alive. He wondered what the sadistic vermin had in mind.

"Have you taken a look around, gringo?" Delgado asked. "Do you know where we are?"

Despite himself, Fargo raised his head as high as he could and gazed past Delgado and Felipe at the landscape. A knot formed in his gut. Perhaps half a mile away was a mesa. Everywhere else was flat, arid ground.

Delgado laughed, thoroughly enjoying himself. "Si, gringo. You are in the Jornada del Muerto. We left Adobe Wells last night after Pedro knocked you out. I'm afraid he hit you harder than he intended, and you've been unconscious for about eighteen hours."

Fargo licked his lips. "Let me guess. You aim to dump me somewhere without any water or food."

"You are a smart man, gringo."

The consequences were obvious. Fargo rested his cheek against the Ovaro and struggled to clear his head, to get the pain under control.

"I have another surprise in store for you," Delgado said, "but I don't want to spoil it." He unfastened his water bag from around his saddle horn, opened the bag, and raised it to his lips. The liquid seeped out of the corners of his mouth as he gulped greedily. Then he made a show of wiping his mouth with the back of his hand and smacking his lips. "You have no idea how good this tastes, gringo." He extended the bag toward Fargo. "Care for a drink?"

"I'd rather have a gun," Fargo said. He shifted his right leg, trying to determine if the Arkansas toothpick was still concealed in his boot. He couldn't tell.

47

"We've decided to keep your weapons," Delgado said. "They will bring a good price back in Albuquerque. So will your horse and saddle."

Fargo hoped the hardcase *would* be stupid enough to sell his things there. Bannister just might get wind of the sale. On second thought, though, he knew there was little Bannister would be able to do. Suspicion wasn't enough to justify an arrest. The lawman would need a body or a witness. Barring those, maybe Bannister would avenge him for the sheer hell of it, would goad Delgado into going for his gun and kill him. He grinned at the notion. Why did desperate men always clutch at straws?

"You find this funny?" Delgado asked in surprise. He replaced the water bag over the saddle horn, moved closer, and leaned down.

Sensing what would happen next, Fargo braced himself for the blow. Delgado backhanded him across the face, causing exquisite anguish to flare in his head. His senses swam for a moment.

"When will you learn, *estúpido*?" Delgado hissed. "No one laughs at me. Ever."

Fargo couldn't resist the temptation. "Looked in a mirror lately?" Another blow slammed into his head, then a third, a fourth, and more. Dizziness caught him in a whirlpool, spinning the world around and around and sucking him down into its ebony depths. That was the last he remembered.

Why wouldn't Grace let him sleep?

Fargo felt someone shaking him by the front of his shirt. For an instant he imagined himself back in the Fairmont Hotel, asleep in bed beside the beautiful blonde. Then, in a bitter rush, his memory returned.

"Wake up, gringo!"

He opened his eyes to find Delgado standing over him, smirking. He was flat on his back on the ground, and now his ankles as well as his wrists were securely tied.

"It's time we were leaving you," Delgado said, turning. His companions were mounted and waiting behind him. He walked to his horse, swung up, and adjusted his sombrero. "It will be night soon and we have a long ride back to Adobe Wells."

Fargo almost laughed aloud, elated at their mistake. They hadn't taken him far enough into the Jornada del Muerto. Had they gone another day or so, it might have been impossible for him to make it safely out of the desert on foot. But now he stood a prayer, a chance of surviving even without water.

"I know we haven't brought you very far," Delgado said, as if he could read Fargo's thoughts. "But to go any farther would be too risky for us. So now you are on your own."

Moving his legs just a bit, Fargo discovered the knife was where it should be. The rope had been wrapped around the outside of his boot, increasing the pressure of the hilt against his ankle. He couldn't wait for them to leave so he could free himself.

"Did I say alone?" Delgado said with a twisted smile. "Not quite, gringo." He nodded to the south. "We saw smoke signals a while ago, not more than a mile or two off. And we both know what that means, don't we?"

Fargo looked southward. There was a mesa approximately a mile away and another not quite two miles from them.

Delgado suddenly pulled his revolver and cocked the hammer. "Do you know how well sound carries in the desert, gringo?" Laughing, he pointed the gun into the air and squeezed off four slow shots, spacing them so the blasts would clearly roll across the bleak expanse of parched terrain in all directions. Then he holstered the gun. "Can you guess what will happen now?"

Fargo didn't need to guess. He knew.

"I will tell you," Delgado said. "Gunfire draws Indians as honey draws bears. They will come to see what all the shooting was about, and when they find you—" He stopped and beamed.

"I would not want to be in your boots, hombre," Felipe chimed in.

"Adios, gringo," Delgado said, and wheeled his horse. The rest followed his example, and together they galloped back the way they had come, heading for Adobe Wells, clouds of dust rising on their heels.

Grunting, his head lanced with spasms, Fargo succeeded in sitting up. The sun hung over the western horizon, on the verge of disappearing. He studied those mesas again. Rising from the nearest one was a thin column of white smoke.

Delgado had told the truth, damn his black heart!

Fargo forced himself to wait until the four men were nearly out of sight before he tried to insert his fingers into his boot. It wouldn't do to have one of them look back and catch a glint of sunlight off the knife blade. He needn't have worried. The rope was so tight he couldn't get his fingers underneath. Frustrated, he set to work on the knots but found he could barely get a nail into them. Freeing himself would take much longer than he'd anticipated.

He glanced at the smoke signal. If he took too long, he could forget about dying of thirst. The desert would be the least of his problems. Those Indians would dispose of him in any one of a dozen brutal ways, and each would have him begging them to end his life before they were done. They might skin him alive, or stake him out in the sun, or gouge out his eyes and leave him to wander aimlessly, all methods the Apaches and Navahos had used in the past on white intruders into their territory.

Since he wasn't making any headway on the ankle rope, he raised his forearms and attacked the knots on the rope around his wrists. Whoever had tied them had done an outstanding job. He gripped the upper edge of a small loop and tugged furiously with his teeth. Gradually, after several minutes, the loop budged slightly.

An acute sense of hopelessness gripped him, but he shook it off. Don't think about the smoke signal! he told himself. Don't think about anything but getting the knot undone. Nothing else mattered. He gripped the loop again and strained his jaw muscles until they hurt. Again the loop budged, but not much. Grimly, he applied his teeth to the chore with a vengeance.

Time passed. A gray tinge shrouded the countryside. From the northwest blew a cool breeze.

Fargo hardly noticed. His lips and gums became raw and sore, but still he yanked and gnawed, refusing to admit defeat. The salty taste of blood touched his tongue, but he continued. His jaw and neck hurt terribly, yet he persisted. And at long last, when only a thin golden halo was all that remained of the sun and a few stars shone overhead, he loosened the last of the knots and the rope fell to the dirt.

His wrists were torn and bleeding, his fingers numb. That

didn't stop him from at once applying his fingers to the knots on the ankle rope. He broke the corner of a fingernail off, grimaced, and tried again. Soon it would be too dark to see the knot. He must undo it quickly.

He happened to glance toward the mesa and was glad to see the signaling had stopped. Then his eyes drifted lower and an icy chill rippled down his spine.

There were horsemen approaching!

Startled, he counted eight in all, halfway between the nearest mesa and where he sat. The twilight prevented him from being certain, but he guessed they were Indians; none appeared to be wearing hats and a few appeared to be nearly naked. He doubted they had spotted him yet. That would soon change.

He renewed his assault on the knots, then wedged his fingers under the rope and wrenched savagely. A little slack developed, giving him added leverage, and he used it to firm his hold. His shoulder muscles bunched into compact cords as he pulled with all his might, and he felt as if his fingers were going to be torn from his hands. The rope loosened some more, a half inch or so, and he squeezed two fingers into his boot and gripped the hilt between them. He tried to get the knife out, but there still wasn't enough room.

The Indians were drawing closer by the second.

Frantic, Fargo slid both hands under the rope again and hauled on it as hard as he could. Gradually additional slack developed, and when he finally judged the space to be adequate he tried to extract the throwing knife. This time he squeezed the tooth-pick all the way out.

Working swiftly, he cut the rope, then rose into a crouch. The Indians were a quarter of a mile off, vague forms in the gathering twilight. He glanced around and saw nowhere to take cover except for a few clusters of cactus. Keeping stooped over, the cut-up ropes in his hand, he dashed toward the cactus, going to the last cluster and dropping down behind a squat, spiny plant.

He hugged the earth, the Arkansas toothpick clutched in his right hand, and listened to the drumming of the horses' hooves. Easing his head to the left, he peeked past the edge of the cactus and saw that eight riders were within a hundred yards of his position. There could be no doubt they were Indians. Despite the encroaching darkness, he distinguished their flowing hair and the lances a few of them carried.

The Indians never slowed. They passed within ten feet of the spot where he'd removed the ropes and pressed onward without a sideways glance.

Fargo grinned in relief, but it turned out he was a bit premature because the very next moment one of the warriors reined up and looked back.

7

The rest of the Indians followed suit.

Wishing he could burrow a hole like a badger, Fargo tensed and girded himself to make a desperate bid for his life. The warrior who had looked back now swung his horse around and came slowly toward the cactus clusters, his head swiveling from side to side, as if he was searching for something but had no clear-cut idea of what it was he sought. Fargo figured the warrior had sensed something wasn't right; he'd known Indians who possessed an uncanny intuition where danger was concerned, intuition no doubt honed by a lifetime of living in the wild and dealing with threats to life and limb on a regular basis. He waited to see if the man would come close enough to detect his prone form, holding his breath, his every nerve tingling.

One of the other warriors said something, another chimed in a comment, and the warrior nearing the cactus stopped and addressed them.

Fargo knew the language. He'd heard it spoken before, although he knew few of the words. It was Navaho, which meant these warriors composed a Navaho war party, and if they found him they'd kill him. He guessed that the others wanted to go on and the one who had turned was trying to explain why he had stopped. Then a couple laughed, and the intuitive one rejoined them. Off they went, moving rapidly, apparently eager to reach their destination.

Fargo was alone in the vast expanse of the Jornada del Muerto. He rose to his knees and inhaled the cool air. The desert cooled down quickly at night, and by morning would be quite chilly, which would make traveling on foot a pleasure compared to what it was like during the day. And he must walk as far as he could before sunrise, then find a nook to hole up in until tomorrow night. That was the first unwritten law of desert survival: Unless you had no other choice, you should always travel at night.

He stood, then leaned down to pull the sheath from his boot. He unbuckled his belt, slipped it through the loop in the sheath, and aligned the sheath on his right hip. Since the knife was his only weapon and he might need it at a moment's notice, he wanted it handy. Removing the toothpick from his boot took too much time. He slid the blade into the sheath, patted the hilt, and headed out.

Ascertaining the direction to go was a cinch. He knew the positions of the stars and the constellations well. He found the Big Dipper readily enough. The two stars that formed the front of the dipper were almost in a direct line with the North Star, in effect pointing the way toward Adobe Wells.

He didn't go far before he stopped and removed his spurs. Like most men in the West who spent most of their time on horseback and so needed to wear spurs constantly, he'd learned to tread quietly with them on. When necessary, he could cover ground as silently as an Indian. But over long distances it wasn't practical, and he didn't intend to go clinking across the desert where there were sharp-eared Navahos in the area.

Fargo left them lying in the dust. Spurs were cheap, and he would buy a pair when he reached Albuquerque. The thought prompted him to check his pockets. Naturally, his money was gone, already on its way back to town with Delgado and his bunch. He couldn't wait to run into them again. And he would. No matter how long it took, he aimed to track them down and repay them in kind for what they had done to him.

The notion sustained him as he trudged a mile, then two. As usual, coyotes howled intermittently. Once he heard the screech of a small animal being attacked, then there was silence except for the dull thud of his footsteps. Fortunately, there were few creatures in the desert capable of posing a threat. Cougars and bears preferred the mountains. Wolves were scarce so far south.

His foremost worry was rattlesnakes. Rattlers came out to hunt at night, and if he should blunder onto a sidewinder in the dark and step on it, he'd be a corpse by morning. He tried to avoid sage and mesquite and rocks where the snakes might hide.

His stomach growled, reminding him of how hungry he was, and he ignored the discomfort. Eating wasn't very important. A man could live for weeks without food, but water was altogether different. Three days without water and a person became weak and disoriented, especially if the three days were spent in the sweltering heat of the merciless desert. Holing up during the day would not prevent him from drying up; it would only delay the inevitable.

Occasionally he saw a mesa to the east or west, a huge black flat-topped mountain even more devoid of life than the desert. Toward daylight he would head for one. Quite often there were caves and crevasses at their base, ideal places to curl up and rest out the glaring sun.

He tried to estimate how many miles he must travel before he reached Adobe Wells. If Delgado and his men had ridden all night and then into the afternoon, they could have covered between eighty and one hundred and ten miles, depending on how hard they had pushed their mounts. He doubted they had ridden very fast once the sun rose, which might reduce the total a little. But the sad truth of the matter was that he faced a hike of approximately eighty miles, which he must complete in three days. Covering such a distance in the desert on foot in that amount of time would take a lot of luck.

Fargo's head still hurt. He touched his temple and found a gash where Pedro had struck him. At least he hadn't lost a lot of blood, or his hair would be caked with it. He pressed onward, idly thinking about Grace and Albuquerque and fools who should know better than to take beautiful ladies up on propositions guaranteed to get them killed.

He supposed he'd gone twelve miles when another mesa materialized to the northeast. He hardly gave it a glance. One escarpment looked just like another in the dark. Then he saw the light.

A faint, shimmering flicker of yellowish light flared for several seconds near the bottom of the mesa then disappeared.

Halting in surprise, Fargo scanned the gloomy base, hoping to see the light again. A light meant a fire, which might mean Indians, maybe the Navahos he'd encountered earlier. It also meant that whoever had built the fire had stopped to camp, and if they had horses the mounts would be nearby. He would do anything to get his hands on a horse.

Another brief glow became visible at the same spot.

Fargo had seen enough. He headed for the mesa, his right hand resting on the hilt of his knife. In the next ten minutes the light reappeared twice more. After that, as he neared the base, nothing. Enormous boulders reared in his path, blocking his view, but he hoped to see the light again once he was past them. When that moment arrived, when he stepped around the last boulder and could see the bottom of the mesa clearly, he stopped short in confusion.

Looming high above him, about sixty yards off, was a solid rock wall that rose for hundreds of feet straight into the air. Nowhere was there a hint of light.

How could this be? Fargo asked himself, moving forward. He was certain he had arrived at the proper area. There should be a fire. He scoured the mesa from top to bottom and east to west, in vain. Advancing closer only confirmed the disappointing discovery. Forty yards from the base he halted and slapped his thigh in frustration.

A fire couldn't just vanish into thin air!

He sniffed loudly, trying to detect the acrid scent of smoke, but all he smelled was the dry, earthy aroma of the desert. Either he'd imagined the whole incident or the blows to his head had done more damage than he'd realized. His shoulders slumping in resignation, he pivoted and started to leave, to resume his arduous task.

A soft voice carried in the breeze.

Startled, Fargo crouched and whipped the knife free. He swung around, studying the face of the mesa again, certain the voice came from there. The words had been mere whispers, so vague he hadn't been able to identify the language being spoken. Better to assume the worst, he reckoned, than to blunder into a band of hostiles. So acting on the assumption there were Indians somewhere nearby, he stealthily glided toward the rock wall.

He went twenty yards, then stopped in bewilderment. A strong, cool current of air fanned his face and hair, seemingly coming from the very bottom of the mesa. Puzzled, he crept closer until the mystery was explained.

Concealed in the black shadows was an opening the size of a log cabin, the mouth of a cave, perhaps. From a distance it blended into the surrounding darkness and gave the illusion of being part of the solid wall. Close up, it was an irregular, inky shape.

Holding the knife low, Fargo slanted to the right of the opening and pressed his back to the stone. The refreshing air current became stronger. The whispering was briefly repeated. He inched his head out until he could see inside, then gaped in astonishment.

Much of the interior of the mesa consisted of a mammoth cavern, its recesses shrouded in gloom. To the right, seemingly carved out of the stone itself, rose a stupendous honeycomb of two-story houses piled in an orderly arrangement from the lowest to the highest, rising from the cavern floor to the vaulted roof. Wooden ladders afforded access to terraces on top of many of the dwellings.

Fargo had never seen the like. He spotted a large fire on top of one of the highest terraces and the reddish glow of other fires in several of the uppermost houses, and wondered if it had been a reflection of that combined light that had lured him to the mesa. There was no sign of the occupants, who might all be indoors, but he wasn't about to take reckless chances. He checked and double-checked the area near the entrance, figuring there would be guards, but found no one.

Doubling over, he padded around the edge of the entrance and cut to the right, staying next to the wall where the shadows obscured his movements. Suddenly a figure appeared on the terrace where the fire blazed, and Fargo halted and crouched even lower. The figure looked out over the cavern, then stretched.

So there was a guard. The height was too great for Fargo to observe details, but there was no mistaking the rifle in the man's hands. It glinted dully in the firelight. The figure moved back out of sight seconds later.

Fargo advanced toward one of the ladders. He scoured the cavern floor for horses but spied none. Maybe, he speculated, there was a hidden chamber off the main cavern where the mounts were kept. All he had to do was grab one of the people living up there and get him to talk.

He came to the ladder and gripped one of the rungs. The whole ladder wobbled, creaking as if about to fall to pieces, so he dropped the rung and stepped back. Climbing it would be impossible. The thing must be ancient. But then how had those people in the upper dwellings scaled the buildings?

Fargo moved to the left, never straying more than a step or two from the lower stone walls, none of which contained doors or windows. Every ladder he came across was in the same decrepit state. He wondered who had built this strange place, and then recollected stories he'd heard about the peaceful Pueblo Indians who lived much farther to the west in adobe structures a lot like these. Had the Pueblos lived here at one time? Or had their ancestors? Even more to the point, who was living here now?

Halfway along the lower dwellings he found the answer to at least one of his questions. Dangling from the terrace twenty feet above was a thick rope, knotted at intervals to provide a better grip. Had he not been running his hand over the smooth stones, he would have missed it. He raised the toothpick to his mouth, clamped his teeth on the hilt, and grabbed hold of the rope. Then he started pulling himself upward hand over hand.

Fargo expected to be challenged or to have another guard pop up at the top and open fire. Oddly, he reached the terrace without any difficulty and scrambled over the rim, lying on his stomach as he listened to learn if he'd been spotted. Silence shrouded the cliff dwellings.

He glanced up. Eighty feet above him was the terrace where the fire blazed. There were plenty of ladders on the intervening levels, but he suspected there was another rope somewhere, since only a fool would use those rickety affairs. Rising, he searched the terrace. At one side was a doorway into a dwelling.

With his knife at the ready, Fargo eased inside. There was barely enough light to see by. His hand brushed a wall and he felt dust cover his skin, indicating no one had lived there for a long time. There was no furniture, nothing except a few vases in a corner. He backed out and craned his neck to see the next terrace, trying to figure out how to get up there.

Stumped, he went to the edge and knelt beside the rope, curious as to how it had been attached. To his amazement, he found that a picket pin, of the kind used to tether horses at night when in wild country, had been pounded at an angle into the roof and then the rope had been secured around the pin.

Just then, from below, arose the sound of footsteps and someone grunting. Fargo flattened and moved away from the rim into the room containing the vases. He didn't have long to wait before a head appeared, and a bearded man wearing a white hat climbed onto the terrace. The man turned, dropped to one knee, and began hauling the rope up.

Fargo rose and closed on the stranger, stepping slowly, intending to take him alive. He didn't make a sound, but when he still had five feet to go the bearded hombre abruptly stiffened and whirled, his arms at his sides as if he was holding something. Fargo leaped, executing a diving tackle, only the man was faster. He saw a circular object sweep up and out, and he was in midair when a bucketful of water caught him squarely in the face, temporarily blinding him and throwing him off balance. He landed hard on his elbows and knees near the edge, . and before he could wipe the water from his eyes and rise, the bearded stranger pounced on his back.

8

Iron knees gouged into Fargo's shoulder blades and strong hands grasped his chin from behind, wrenching backward in an attempt to snap his neck. He lashed rearward with the knife, felt the point connect, and heard a yelp of pain. One of the hands slipped off his chin, and by sharply twisting to the right, Fargo was able to flip his assailant onto the terrace. Surging upright, he saw the bearded man holding his right forearm and trying to stand. Fargo kicked, his left leg sweeping up and out, and the sole of his foot slammed into the man's mouth and knocked him down.

"You heathen devil!" the bearded man cried, sputtering, and went to rise.

"Hold it, mister!" Fargo barked, swinging the knife overhead to throw it if need be. "I'm no Indian."

The man froze, his hands on the terrace, his legs bent. "You're not?" he exclaimed in astonishment.

"Hell, no," Fargo said. "Take a good look."

"You don't talk like no Injun," the man said, tilting his head and peering intently at Fargo. "I'll be," he said at last. "You are white."

Fargo lowered the knife. As near as he could tell, the man was unarmed.

"With that dark hair of yours and those buckskins, you sure had me fooled," the man said. "My name is Amos Chilton. Who might you be?"

"Skye Fargo."

"Mind if I stand, Mr. Fargo? I won't cause no more trouble."

"Be my guest."

Chilton straightened, clutching his right arm. "You stuck me good. I'll need tending so I don't bleed to death."

"I didn't want to hurt you," Fargo told him, and slid the

blade into its sheath. "But you were about to tear my head off."

"I thought you were one of those skulking Navahos," Chilton said bitterly. "They usually leave us alone at night, which is why I was on my way back from the spring with water at this hour. During the day there's always a few hanging around, trying to pick us off. We can't leave the upper levels then."

"You're not alone, I gather."

"There's eight of us, all told. Four men and four women. We were part of a wagon train that was attacked by Navahos about four weeks ago. Our brethren were killed or abducted."

Suddenly Fargo understood. "You're Shakers."

Chilton blinked. "Yes. How did you know?"

"It's a long story," Fargo told him, moving forward. "I'll tell you after we see about taking care of that arm. You're bleeding bad," he said, and pointed at black splotches at the man's feet.

"Follow me," Chilton said, hastening through the doorway.

Fargo did, and saw the man go through another doorway on the other side. He quickly overtook the Shaker and stuck to his heels as they went the lengths of five more chambers, barely able to see a yard in front of him the whole time, then halted under an opening in the roof. "You sure know your way around this place," he commented.

"We've had almost a month to explore every nook and cranny," Chilton said, stepping to the right-hand wall. He leaned down and said, "Give me a hand with this, will you?"

Moving over, Fargo found him trying to lift a ladder. Unlike the others, this one was sturdy. "Let me," he offered, and positioned it under the opening, leaning the upper end against the edge.

"We used some of our rope to repair this one," Chilton said, beginning to climb, favoring his right hand. "When we pull this up, the savages can't get near us."

Fargo followed, seeing shadows dance overhead. When he emerged, he was much closer to the fire above, which was considerably larger than he'd estimated. "What do you use for firewood?" he asked.

"Ladders, wood from our wagons, dry cactus, whatever we can find," Chilton said. He headed for yet another doorway.

"Are your wagons near here?"

"About a mile due east," Chilton said. "We take our lives in our hands every time we sneak out of the cavern. We never know when the Navahos might ambush us."

They crossed four rooms and stopped under a square opening in the roof. A rope hung down from the level above.

"I don't rightly see how I can climb this one with my bum arm," Chilton said, staring apprehensively upward.

"I'll go first and try to haul you up," Fargo proposed.

"There's a better way. You don't need to do it alone," Chilton said, and cupped his left hand to his mouth. "Brother Caleb! Can you hear me?"

A man promptly responded. "What do you need, Brother Amos?"

"I need help. I've met a gent who is going to climb up the rope. Don't shoot him, you hear?"

"Send him up."

Fargo quickly scaled the rope to find a lean man armed with a rifle standing nearby. It was the guard he'd seen earlier. "Howdy," he said in greeting, and grasped the rope firmly. "Amos can't make it up on his own. Give me a hand, will you?"

Rather reluctantly, Caleb put the rifle down and stood behind Fargo. "Why can't he climb by himself?" he asked.

"Because I stabbed him," Fargo explained, and leaned over the opening. "Tie the rope around your chest and tug when you're ready," he called down.

Caleb coughed. "You stabbed him?"

"Get ready," Fargo said. When the tug came, he glanced at the lean Shaker and nodded. "Pull for all you're worth." His arms straining, he heaved. Chilton was heavier than he'd expected and the progress was slow, but working together he and Caleb finally lifted their burden to the terrace.

"Thank you," Chilton said, rising and unfastening the rope. "Now I'll wake up the others and introduce you."

"What is going on?" Caleb asked, retrieving the rifle. "Who is this man, Brother Amos? Where did he come from? Is it safe to bring him up here?"

"Don't get excited," Chilton cautioned. "We're in no danger

from him." He moved toward a dwelling well lit by a fire within. "This way, Mr. Fargo."

A spacious room had been thoroughly cleaned. Spread on the floor were a number of blankets for bedding, and piled against one wall were supplies evidently salvaged from their wagons. Two men were in the act of getting dressed. A gray-haired man who was hitching up his black pants glanced up and scowled.

"What in tarnation is all the yelling about, Brothers?"

"We have a visitor," Chilton announced, and stepped aside.

Both men gawked at the sight of Fargo and rattled off a string of questions until Chilton motioned for quiet.

"We'll know all there is to know in a bit," Chilton told them, then held up his right forearm so they could see the blood. "Right now I need doctoring. Would you rouse the sisters, Brother Paul, and fetch them?"

"Right away," the elderly Shaker said, slipping into a flannel shirt. He spun and departed out a door on the left.

"You leave the women in another room?" Fargo asked, thinking of what would happen to them should the Navahos gain entry to the upper levels.

"Certainly," Chilton answered. "It would be improper and indecent for us to share sleeping quarters with our beloved sisters of the faith."

"Do they have any weapons?" Fargo asked.

Chilton shook his head. "They refuse to bear arms, even against the savages who took the lives of those we loved so dearly."

Caleb nodded. "They would rather be ravaged than violate one of the Commandments and take another life. For that matter, neither will Brother Paul or Brother Thomas, here, kill another human." He nodded at the fourth man, a youngster of seventeen or eighteen who couldn't take his wide eyes off Fargo.

Fargo nodded at the rifle Caleb held. "I take it you don't share their feelings?"

"I did once," Caleb said, frowning, "before the savages swarmed over us. But when I saw Brother Shafter slain, I lost my head. I took three lives." He hefted the rifle distastefully. "Now I'm bound for Hell. I might as well do what little I can to protect my brothers and sisters."

Chilton looked at Fargo. "He never should have brought that gun along. But he always was the one for trusting more in his own arm than the arm of the Lord."

"You came all this way from Ohio with just one rifle?" Fargo said in disbelief.

"Yes," Chilton said, and his eyes narrowed. "How do you know we came from Ohio? Who *are* you?"

"Let's wait for the ladies," Fargo proposed, going over to squat beside the fire. It felt good to warm his hands. He noticed a small tin containing jerky and a partially filled jug of water near the wall. "Mind if I help myself?" he asked.

"Take your fill, friend," Chilton said.

Greedily, Fargo gulped from the jug, then picked up the tin and crammed two sticks of jerky into his mouth, chewing noisily. Saliva filled his mouth. He grabbed another stick, then hesitated, struck by a thought. "How much food do you have left?" he asked.

"Just the jerky in that can," Caleb replied.

"Oh," Fargo said, assailed by guilt, realizing they would have let him finish the last of their food and not uttered a protest. He put the can back. Suddenly something occurred to him. Chilton had told him there were four men and four women in the group, when originally there had been eight women and six men, which meant half of the women must have been taken by the Navahos. What if Gretchen Davenport was one of them?

"I really shouldn't criticize Brother Caleb for bringing his rifle," Chilton said. "I'm just as guilty of sin as he is. I struck one of the heathens with my fist." He paused. "And I would have broken your neck if you hadn't stopped me."

"It's been hard trying to protect the others," Caleb added. "The two of us have gotten very little sleep."

"They should lend a hand," Fargo said.

"Oh, no, friend," Chilton disagreed. "Unlike Brother Caleb and myself, they have been true to our beliefs. I admire them for their unflinching faith. I only wish mine was half as strong as theirs."

"Their faith could get them killed."

"If so, they will die gloriously, as did Brother Shafter," Caleb proudly defended them. "They will enter the hereafter with unblemished souls."

Fargo didn't bother to debate the point, and he wasn't about to criticize their religious beliefs. It seemed, though, as if he'd gone from the frying pan into the fire. Where before he had only his own hide to watch out for, now he must try to save eight people from a war party of Navahos when only two of the eight could be counted on to help out in a fight.

Voices sounded, and a moment later Brother Paul returned with the women in tow.

Turning toward the door, Fargo couldn't believe his eyes when four lovely ladies entered. He'd expected at least half of them to be past their prime, but all four were young and radiant. To his immense relief, Gretchen Davenport was foremost among them, a blonde like her older sister with the same sparkling blue eyes but a thinner figure and a demure expression. Behind her came two brunettes and a woman with raven tresses. All four wore similar dresses—blue with large white collars and hems down to their shoes. All four wore white shawls over their shoulders. He smiled at them and went to doff his hat, then recollected it had been lost.

"Sisters," Chilton declared, "we're sorry to disturb your rest at such a late hour, but as you can see, the Lord has sent us someone who might be able to help us in our dire need."

"Now hold on, mister," Fargo interrupted, not certain he liked the notion of being considered an instrument of the Almighty. "I'm here because Grace Davenport hired me to find her sister."

"Grace?" Gretchen blurted, coming up to him and gripping his wrist. "She cared enough to do that for me?"

"Why wouldn't she?" Fargo rejoined. "I reckon she cares for you as much as any sister does for another."

"We haven't been close in so long—" Gretchen said, and left the statement unfinished as tears welled in her eyes and she bowed her head.

Caleb pointed at Chilton. "One of you should be tending to Brother Amos. He's been stabbed in the right arm."

The other three women immediately converged on the

wounded Shaker. They examined his arm, decided the wound would heal with time and proper care, and diligently went to work cleaning and bandaging it.

All this time Fargo stood silently, Gretchen's warm hand still on his wrist. She seemed dazed by her sister's concern, and he didn't fully understand the reason why. Tears trickled down her cheeks and she sniffed now and then. When the doctoring was completed, Fargo became the sole object of attention for everyone else in the room. He gently removed his wrist from Gretchen's grasp and faced them. "My name is Skye Fargo, and I'll try to get you out of this mess if you'll let me."

"What is this business about Sister Gretchen's relative hiring you?" one of the brunettes inquired.

"Who are you?" Fargo asked.

"Oh, my apologies," the brunette said. "I'm Sister Joan." She turned to the other brunette. "This is Sister Ruth." Then she nodded at the woman with black hair. "And this is Sister Naomi."

"My pleasure, ladies," Fargo said, and launched into a short explanation of his meeting with Grace Davenport and his run-in with the Delgado bunch at Adobe Wells. He concluded with, "So there I was, hiking across the godforsaken desert, when I saw a light and found this cavern."

"The hand of our Lord brought you to us," Chilton said. "You are our deliverer."

Fargo stepped to the left and leaned his back against the wall. After all he'd been through, his body needed rest. Every muscle ached. The crackling fire was so inviting that he wanted to curl up beside it and sleep for a week. "I'd like to hear what happened to you folks after you left Albuquerque. I know you met an old prospector at Adobe Wells, then headed into the Jornada del Muerto."

"Yes," Chilton confirmed. "Seeking the paradise Brother Shafter had promised us we would find here."

"No one in his right mind would ever call the desert a paradise," Fargo said. "Where did he get such a crazy idea?"

"It wasn't so crazy, friend," Chilton said sadly. "And before you think badly of him, you should understand his reason for coming." He paused. "As you are aware, we are Shakers. I don't know whether you know it, but for many years the Shakers have been persecuted for their beliefs. In public we have often been insulted to our faces, or assaulted. Whenever we ventured from our farm in Ohio, the townspeople would scorn us. Living there became unbearable. So Brother Shafter brought us to this Territory in the hope of starting over and in a land where we could live as we wished in peace. His motives were unselfish."

"But why *here*?" Fargo wanted to know.

Brother Paul answered. "Because of the man who came to Dayton and spoke on his travels around the world, friend."

"What man?" Fargo asked.

"His name was Garforth," Paul said. "He'd been just about everywhere. Europe. Africa. Asia. And he spent a year in this region, making sketches and keeping a journal of everything he saw, heard, and did."

Fargo nodded in understanding. There were a number of men, and a few women, who made a decent living by going around the country lecturing on the exotic and unusual places they'd visited. Invariably individuals who loved to travel, they went from town to town much as would an itinerant preacher or a salesman but making much more money from folks eager to hear about strange countries and stranger people. They would draw in the curious from miles around for each talk. And after eight months to a year on the lecture circuit, they would use their earnings to satisfy their wanderlust once again. When they ran out of funds, they would return to the States for another round of lectures.

"Brother Shafter went into Dayton to hear Garforth speak. During the talk, Garforth told about tales of lost cities in the Southwest, about cities once inhabited by Indians but now deserted, even though there was plenty of water and game to be had. He said that no one knows why the cities were deserted, not even the experts."

Fargo put two and two together. "So Shafter decided to find one of these cities and claim it as his own."

"Our own," Paul corrected. "A home where we would never again face bigotry, never again be subjected to persecution."

"But you still haven't told me why you came to the Jornada del Muerto," Fargo noted. "There are other remote regions you could have picked."

"Brother Shafter went up and spoke to Garforth after the lecture," Paul detailed. "Garforth mentioned hearing from his Indian guide about a lost city in this very area. Because of the hazards, Garforth never investigated the claim. The Indian had disclosed that the city was hidden in a cavern in a mesa with a huge rock outcropping on its eastern side." He glanced at the doorway. "We had spent five days going from mesa to mesa, trying to find the lost city, when we spied this mesa and headed toward it. That was when the Navahos jumped us."

Fargo's brow knit in thought. In a way these Shakers reminded him of the Mormons. In order to escape similar harassment, the Mormons had trekked all the way from Illinois to the Great Salt Lake valley, at the time an uninhabited wilderness but now part of the Territory of Utah. "Tell me about the Navahos," he prompted.

Chilton took up the narrative. "There were eleven of them. They rode up to us in broad daylight, blocking our way. Brother Shafter stepped forward to greet them, to let them know we would not harm them, and that was when one of the savages shot him in the chest." His voice lowered. "Brother Shafter didn't fall, however. He again tried to convince them our intentions were peaceful. Another savage sent an arrow into him, and he dropped."

"We must not call them savages," Sister Joan said. "They are just as much God's children as we are."

Caleb made a sound that resembled the bleat of an angry male goat. "You'll never convince me of that, Sister. Not after what happened." He looked at Fargo. "The Navahos yelled and waved their weapons and rode in among us. Two of our brothers were slain right away, even though they were unarmed. Four of our sisters were taken off the wagons. They stole our horses. And worst of all, they treated us with contempt because we wouldn't defend ourselves. Some of them laughed as they went about their grisly work." He scowled at the memory. "That was when I grabbed my rifle and started firing. Caught them by surprise, I'll tell you. I killed three of the devils before the rest galloped off.''

"And I knocked one from my wagon,'' Chilton added.

"How did you wind up in here?'' Fargo asked.

"We knew the Navahos would be back, so we decided to find cover,'' Caleb said. "The nearest mesa was this one. You can't imagine how happy we were when we found the cavern.''

"We've been here ever since,'' Paul stated.

Fargo turned to Chilton. "Where is the spring?''

"At the back of the cavern, west of the dwellings. It's not very deep, but it's filled our needs. I don't believe the Navahos know it's there.''

"We've killed some lizards,'' Caleb said, "which is why our store-bought food has lasted so long.''

Gretchen Davenport finally joined the conversation, her sniffling under control. "Now we're about at our wit's end, Mr. Fargo,'' she declared. "I had about given up hope of ever leaving this horrid place alive.''

Fargo rubbed his forehead and sighed. So far these pilgrims had been extremely fortunate, but their luck couldn't hold forever. How was he going to get them out alive? If they tried to hike out, the Navahos would be on them before they went five miles. And even if they somehow eluded the Navahos, there was the question of how to cover the seventy or eighty miles of harsh terrain without succumbing to the heat. "Do you have water bags or canteens?''

"One water bag,'' Gretchen responded. "We keep it in our room.''

Fargo brightened at the news. With strict rationing, they just might be able to reach Adobe Wells. "Then we have a prayer, after all,'' he commented.

"Of doing what?'' Sister Joan inquired.

"Reaching civilization, what else?'' Fargo retorted.

"You're assuming that all of us want to go back,'' Joan said stiffly.

"You don't?''

"No,'' Joan stated. "Some of us want to stay and see Brother Shafter's dream bear fruit. If we can persuade the Navahos that we're friendly, they'll leave us alone. Then we can transform these cliff dwellings into the Eden he envisioned.''

Fargo studied the others and saw a few nod in agreement. ''Just so I get this straight, how many of you want to stay here besides her?''

Ruth, Naomi, Paul, and Thomas all answered in the affirmative.

Amazed at their stubbornness, Fargo gestured angrily in the direction of the cavern opening. ''You folks don't seem to realize those Navahos will never make peace with you. They want your hair. It's as plain and simple as that. Didn't the deaths of Shafter and the others teach you anything?''

''It taught me,'' Caleb said.

Joan refused to be influenced by Fargo's logic. ''We must try harder to convince them, that's all. Just this evening we discussed having one or two of us go out to talk to them tomorrow morning.''

''Whoever goes won't come back,'' Fargo predicted.

''You're saying that to try to scare us,'' Joan said.

''I'm saying it because it's true,'' Fargo responded, and motioned at their meager pile of supplies. ''Besides, how can you think about staying when you don't have enough grub left to last a week and most of your supplies have been taken by the Navahos? How long do you reckon you'll last?''

''If we make peace, we can send someone to obtain more supplies,'' Joan countered obstinately.

Frowning, Fargo scanned the tranquil faces of the five who wanted to remain, then muttered, ''It's true what they say. You can educate fools, but you sure as hell can't make them think.''

''There is no need to be insulting,'' Joan said.

Fargo didn't know what to say to convince her she was being an idiot. He'd automatically assumed all of them would leap at the chance to get out of there. This complicated the situation terribly. He wasn't about to stay, yet he couldn't up and leave them to their gory fate. ''Damn,'' he said irritably, and moved over beside the fire, turning his back on the Shakers.

''We must hold a meeting,'' Paul announced.

''In our room,'' Joan said.

Fargo listened to them leave, too angry to speak. He stared into the flickering flames and pondered his options. If the five who refused to go wouldn't change their minds, he could lead the rest back to Albuquerque and report those who stayed to the Army. Maybe the military would send a patrol to forcibly take the dunderheads back.

His immediate problem was the Navahos. The war party must come from one of their settlements to the northwest. Chilton had told him that during the day there were always a few around, keeping watch. Where did the rest go? And why didn't they stay in the cavern after dark? He tried putting himself in their moccasins and came to several conclusions.

First, the warriors were going to wait the Shakers out. The Indians knew that eventually the whites would run out of food and come down. Why should they needlessly risk their lives in scaling the terraces when those they wanted would make it easy for them?

Second, the members of the war party must be making regular trips between their hogans and the cavern. They wouldn't stay away from their families for weeks at a stretch. Perhaps they were working in shifts. But then why had he seen eight earlier? Were they planning to mount an all-out attack after all?

Third, they must be afraid to enter the cavern once night fell. A tribal taboo would account for their absence between sunset and sunrise. Indians were quite superstitious, and the Navahos might believe evil spirits dwelled in the ancient buildings.

Fargo heard someone enter the room and glanced around.

"May I join you?" Gretchen Davenport asked nervously.

"Sure," Fargo said, then inquired, "Why aren't you with the others?"

"I have nothing to contribute. They all know where I stand," Gretchen said, coming over and standing on his right side. "I don't want to stay, Mr. Fargo. If you're going back, then I'd like you to take me along."

"What about Chilton and Caleb?"

"I can't say," Gretchen told him. "They want to go, but I don't know if they can bring themselves to leave the others behind." She gazed sadly at the fire. "Once, I would have been just like Joan. But after I saw Brother Shafter killed and our sisters taken by those grinning savages, something happened inside of me. My faith will never be the same.''

Fargo saw turmoil in the set of her face and wished he could offer words of wisdom to comfort her. But he was hardly the one to be advising anyone about religious matters.

"I'm quitting the Shakers," Gretchen said.

"Your sister told me you were happy as one."

"Was," Gretchen emphasized, and looked into his eyes. "I've had a lot of time to think since Brother Shafter died, Mr. Fargo. I've realized I could die anytime, just as he did. I've come to see that I have a lot of living to do, a lot of lost time to make up for. There are things I've never done that I'd like to do before I pass away."

Fargo shifted his feet. Was she saying what he thought she was saying? He felt her hand slip into his and give it a gentle squeeze.

"So many things," she said.

9

Fargo awakened with the smell of smoke in his nostrils. He sat up, memories of the night before returning in a rush. He remembered talking to Gretchen for over an hour, hearing about her troubled childhood. Not having a mother had made her miserable, even more so when she'd learned, at the age of seven, that her mother had died in childbirth. Her birth. She'd felt overwhelming guilt, thinking that she was somehow to blame. To soothe her guilt, she'd turned to religion and eventually wound up a Shaker.

He glanced to his right and saw her sleeping on the other side of the smoldering fire, lying on her back, her features quite lovely in repose, her bosom gently rising and falling. Instead of going back to the women's quarters, she'd simply lain down right there when she'd grown too weary to stay awake.

Fargo stood, gratified that the pain in his head was nearly gone. He looked at the doorway to the terrace and spotted the mouth of the cavern far below. Sunlight streamed inside. He went out.

"Morning, friend."

Fargo turned to the left. Brother Caleb stood near the edge, his rifle cradled in his arms, morosely staring at the cavern floor.

"Morning," Fargo answered. "Did you get any shut-eye?"

"Not a wink. Almost dozed off a few times, though. Since Amos was hurt, I offered to stay on guard the entire night."

"How did the meeting go?" Fargo asked. He'd been mildly surprised that none of the other Shakers had returned before he'd finally dozed off.

"Not good, I'm afraid. They wouldn't listen to me."

"Joan and the rest are still fixing to stay?"

Caleb nodded. "That's not the worst of it. They voted to

attempt to make peace with the Navahos again. Joan and Paul volunteered to go find the Indians and talk to them.''

"Didn't they hear a word I said last night?" Fargo snapped, appalled by their stupidity. "When are they fixing to do it? I must stop them.''

"You're too late," Caleb said, and pointed at the entrance. "There hasn't been any sign yet of the Navahos this morning, so Joan and Paul decided to go out and look around the mesa. They left about fifteen minutes ago.''

"The fools!" Fargo roared. In two bounds he was next to Caleb. "I'll need this more than you do," he said, and yanked the rifle free. Then he spun before Caleb could object and hastened to the square opening. He squatted and gripped the rope.

"Mr. Fargo?" Caleb said.

Fargo glanced at him.

"They're good people. They just think everyone is as filled with love as they are. Save them, please.''

Grimly, Fargo swarmed down the rope and rapidly made his way to the lowest row of terraces. The rope that Chilton had used when fetching water from the spring was again dangling to the dirt floor, and he went down it in a rush, the rifle tucked under his left arm, scraping skin off both palms in his haste. He sprinted toward the opening, hoping he wasn't too late.

The gun was a half-stocked percussion plains rifle, a heavy piece notable for reliable accuracy, although not in the same class as his Sharps. He checked it to make sure it was loaded and found a round in the chamber. One shot wasn't much, but it was better than none. If he hadn't been in such an all-fired hurry, he might have thought to ask Caleb for extra ammunition.

An invisible wall of heat hit him yards from the entrance. He slowed, leveled the rifle, and scanned the area outside for sign of the two Shakers or the Navahos. There were plenty of footprints in the dusty soil, most of them made by moccasin-covered feet. He found where Joan and Paul had walked from the cavern, the tracks of their shoes freshly imprinted on top of all the other sign. They had halted a few yards out, then turned to the left and marched along the base of the mesa.

He trailed them, tempted to shout to draw their attention but knowing any yells would also draw the Navahos if the war party was nearby. The pair had stayed close to the high stone wall, Joan in the lead. Tilting his head way back, he could see the top of the escarpment, so high it appeared to be touching the clouds.

Then, faintly, the sluggish, hot breeze carried a scream of terror punctuated by a savage whoop.

Fargo broke into a run, his arms and legs flying. He weaved among large boulders, leaped a narrow gully, and sprinted across an open tract until he came to more boulders. The scream was repeated once. He knew what he would find long before he rounded a bend in the stone wall, churned up a rocky incline, and spotted the figures dozens of yards away. Instantly he dropped flat, dreading he'd been seen, but none of those below had been gazing in his direction.

There were three Navahos, all dismounted, their horses standing patiently off to the west. One stood over the crumpled form of Brother Paul, the elderly Shaker's gray bloody scalp clutched in his left hand, a crimson-coated knife in the other. The second Navaho was behind Sister Joan, holding her wrists firmly, while the third stood in front of her, taunting her while he casually sliced her dress into thin strips. He wasn't being very careful, either, because there were thin streaks of blood on her pale skin.

"Please, I beg you!" Joan was pleading. "Don't do this. We are all children of our Maker. We should treat each other with respect."

Fargo, confounded, raised the rifle to his right shoulder. How could anyone spout words of brotherly love while they were being carved up by hostiles? He sighted on the warrior doing the slicing, smack in the center of the man's head, and when the Navaho elevated the knife for another swipe, he fired.

The bullet was dead on target. Lifted off his feet by the impact, the Navaho was hurled a few feet and landed in a disjointed heap.

The remaining warriors whirled toward the incline. Screeching in rage, the one who had scalped Paul charged.

Fargo shoved upright and sprinted to meet the Navaho midway. He must dispatch them quickly, before it occurred to either of them to ride off for help, or the rest of the war party showed up on their own, having heard the gunshot. Reversing his grip on the plains rifle, he held it like a club and lifted it on high.

Venting a bloodcurdling cry, the Navaho closed. He sprang when eight feet separated them, his knife arm flashing down and out, trying for a chest strike.

Sidestepping, Fargo swung, the rifle a blur as it arced into the side of the Navaho's head and knocked the man onto his stomach on the ground. Fargo took a half-step and delivered a second blow as the warrior tried to rise, the heavy wooden stock catching the Navaho at the nape of the neck, rendering him senseless.

Pivoting, Fargo ran toward the last warrior. He saw Sister Joan lying on her back. The last Navaho now had a tomahawk in his right hand and was rushing forward. There was blood dripping from the tomahawk.

The thought of such a gentle but misguided soul as Sister Joan being brutally slain sent Fargo over the emotional edge. Rage seized him, and he tore into the last Navaho like a madman, swinging furiously, the stock bashing the warrior in the face at the very first blow, stopping the Navaho in his tracks. The next swing caved in the warrior's front teeth, and his knees gave way. The third swing hit the man in the neck, causing him to wheeze as he doubled over, the tomahawk falling from his suddenly weak fingers.

Fargo scooped the weapon up, and in a smooth motion he sank the sharp edge into the top of the Navaho's head, the blade splitting hair, flesh, and bone with ease. The warrior stiffened, arched his back, and voiced a gurgling screech.

"You should have spared her, damn you," Fargo growled, and wrenched the tomahawk loose.

The Navaho pitched onto his face with a thud.

Turning, Fargo ran to Sister Joan. Her blank eyes gazed up at the azure sky, while between them, running from her ruptured cranium, down her forehead, and over her nose to her chin, was a rivulet of blood. He toyed with the notion of burying her, but forgot the idea when one of the Navaho's horses neighed.

Fargo moved toward them. He wedged the tomahawk under

his belt and spoke soothingly, trying to calm the horses so they wouldn't run off. "It's all right. I won't hurt you. Everything is fine." The nearest, a fine stallion, eyed him warily and struck the earth with a front hoof.

Moving at a snail's pace, Fargo drew close enough to grab the animal's Indian-style bridle. Consisting of a length of rope with a lark's-head knot in the middle over the animal's jaw, it was a simple and effective means of controlling a horse. Once he had the rope reins, he vaulted onto the stallion's back and waited to see if it would object. The horse stood still, docile and ready.

With a flick of his legs, Fargo guided the stallion toward the other two animals. He wanted all three. Getting all the Shakers out of the Jornada del Muerto alive would be so much easier. Provided they all agreed to go, that was.

The other horses abruptly raised their heads and looked to the northwest, their ears pricked.

Fargo promptly spied the reason. Sweeping across the desert toward the mesa were five Navahos. Three held bows. Aware there was no time to lose, he goaded the stallion up to the closest horse, or tried to, but both animals bolted, heading for the Navahos. Chasing them would be futile. By the time he could ovetake them, the Navahos would be within bow range, and their warriors were widely reputed to be expert archers.

Angry at being thwarted, Fargo glanced back along the mesa, thinking of the Shakers in the cavern. He stood an excellent chance of outrunning the war party if he was to head into the desert in the opposite direction, but doing so would mean abandoning the Shakers, leaving them to the same hideous fate as Joan's and Paul's, and he couldn't bring himself to do that. Going back might mean his own death, but he would rather die fighting than be branded a coward by his conscience for the rest of his days. It just wasn't in him to run out on folks in dire need.

He lashed the stallion with the long rope reins and rode hard toward the cliff dwellings. As he went over the incline the Navahos vented excited whoops. They were eager to claim his hair. But he was counting on the sight of their three dead companions to delay them momentarily, long enough to give him a comfortable lead so he could reach the cavern in safety.

Fargo checked behind him repeatedly. When he was only forty yards from the cavern entrance the Navahos appeared, shrieking their wrath, hell-bent on his destruction. He entered the cavern and made for the cliff dwellings, surprised to see Caleb, Chilton, and Gretchen standing on the bottom terrace near the rope.

"What happened?" Chilton called down as he halted at the bottom of the wall. "Where are the others?"

"Dead," Fargo bluntly informed them. He stared across the cavern floor into the shadows along the walls. "Quick. Is there anywhere I can hide this horse where the Navahos wouldn't find it?"

"Not that we know of," Chilton replied.

"What about at the spring?" Fargo asked hopefully. After all the trouble he had gone to, he didn't want to give up the animal without a struggle.

"The water is in a crack in the wall. There's barely room for the bucket," Chilton answered.

Fargo heard the shrieks of the Navahos wafting into the mammoth chamber and echoing off the walls. Swinging his left leg over the stallion's broad back, he jumped down and moved to the rope. "Here. Catch this and reload it," he yelled, then hurled the rifle straight up.

Caleb grabbed it easily.

Grasping the rope, his torn palms stinging, Fargo climbed swiftly. He was only a third of the way to the top when the two fastest Navahos burst into the cavern and barreled toward the dwellings. One held a bow, an arrow already notched to the string.

"Hurry!"

Fargo exerted himself to the utmost, his legs swinging underneath him, his shoulders knotted like cords. An arrow streaked out of the air and smacked into the wall within inches of his head, snapping in half when it hit and falling harmlessly to the cavern floor. Gritting his teeth, he reached higher than he should have and felt his grip slipping. For a frantic heartbeat he almost lost his hold. Then he firmed his grasp and continued, listening to the drumming of hooves to his rear. He dared not risk another look with the Navahos so near. Every second was crucial.

"Look out!" Gretchen screamed.

Instinctively Fargo swung to the left, kicking off the wall to gain momentum. Another arrow struck the stone surface at the very spot where he had hung. He climbed higher, but the rim still seemed impossibly far away. From the racket of the clattering hooves, he gathered that the lead Navahos were almost to the wall. The flesh between his shoulder blades prickled. He knew the bowman would not miss a third time.

Then the rifle barrel jutted over the rim and the gun boomed, spitting lead and smoke.

Fargo had to look. The warrior with the bow had taken a slug in the chest and now lay on his side on the floor, convulsing violently. The other Navaho was in the act of vaulting off his horse, and the rest of the war party was galloping toward the structure from which Fargo hung. He ascended even higher. Then, to his consternation, the rope began moving, jerking right and left, and he peered past his boots to see that the bottom of the rope had been seized by the Navaho who had just alighted.

Smirking wickedly, the warrior was trying to shake Fargo off the rope.

10

"Climb!" Gretchen wailed in despair. "Climb! Climb!"

Fargo couldn't. It took all of his strength simply to cling to the rope for dear life as the warrior below whipped it in wolfish abandon. He glanced across the cavern to find that the other Navahos were less than thirty yards off. A bit closer and he was a goner.

The onrushing warriors voiced their war cries.

Feeling himself start to fall, Fargo clamped both knees on the rope, and when that didn't work, when it seemed certain his hands would slip off and down he would go, he did the only other thing he could think of; he bit the rope. He sank his teeth into the tough fibers, and the added pressure was just enough to temporarily prevent him from plummeting.

Howling, the Navaho below redoubled his efforts to shake Fargo off.

Suddenly the rifle poked out from the top of the terrace, the barrel angling down at the Navaho, who let go of the rope and darted to the right, running in a zigzag pattern, trying to make it difficult for the Shaker to hit him.

Fargo took instant advantage of the momentary reprieve. He scaled the rest of the rope at a speed belying his size, and grabbed the edge to haul himself up. Chilton appeared, reaching down with his good arm.

"Let me help, friend."

"Much obliged," Fargo grunted as he clambered onto the terrace and knelt, catching his breath. The Navaho who had tried to shake him off had stopped fifteen yards out and was glaring at them. He glanced at Caleb. "Why didn't you shoot?"

The Shaker chuckled. "The gun is empty," he said. "I didn't have time to reload it, but I figured you could use a hand."

"I owe you," Fargo said, admiring the man's cleverness.

The bluff had saved his hide. But they weren't out of danger yet, not by a long shot. "Get back," he directed, motioning for the others to move away from the lip as the Navahos galloped up to the wall. He hunched low, gripped the rope, and began hauling it up before they could grab it and try to reach the terrace.

An arrow flashed over his head.

Caleb squatted well back from the edge, his fingers flying, reloading the plains rifle.

Fargo had about five feet of rope coiled at his feet when it was nearly torn out of his hands by someone at the bottom end. One of the warriors had grabbed it! He braced his legs, bunched his muscles, and tugged, but the warrior held on. Then more weight was added, and the rope snapped out of his aching hands and was pulled taut. He peeked over the rim.

Three Navahos had hold of the rope. A fourth started to climb.

Drawing back, Fargo pulled the tomahawk out, lifted it on high, and swept the keen edge into the rope. A squawk from below greeted his action as the severed section dropped from view. Another peek showed that the warrior who had tried to climb the rope was lying on top of another man, both bellowing as they struggled to stand. In a moment both men were up. All four gazed upward, their feral features betraying their state of mind. Then they raced to their horses and dashed off toward the entrance, taking all the riderless mounts with them.

Caleb stepped to the rim and tried to get a bead on the fleeing Navahos.

"Save the bullet," Fargo advised, standing. He stared at the dead Indian. Only four of the eight now remained, and he wondered if the rest would ride off for reinforcements or whether they would hover in the vicinity waiting to pick off the Shakers. Suddenly an arm looped around his waist and he looked down into Gretchen's relieved blue eyes.

"I didn't think you'd make it," she said softly.

"That makes two of us," Fargo remarked, and smiled. He didn't quite know what to do about the way she had taken to him. Her comments the previous night had opened up a possibility that he found himself oddly reluctant to explore. Had any other woman given him the hints she had, he would gladly have bedded her on the spot. But Gretchen had an air of innocence about her, no doubt due to her religious background and her association with the Shakers, that made him feel strangely uncomfortable.

"We're safe for the time being," Chilton said. He turned and headed for the doorway. "I'd better tell the others about Sister Joan and Brother Paul. Maybe it will convince them that staying is a hopeless cause."

"I'll stand guard right here," Caleb volunteered. "If the savages show their faces again, I'll fire a shot and everyone can come running."

"You were awake all night," Fargo said. "Are you sure you're up to staying awake a while longer?"

"I'm fine," Caleb said. "Just thinking about being scalped is enough to keep me awake for days."

Gretchen pulled on Fargo's hand. "You must be thirsty after going out in that terrible heat. Come with me and I'll get you some water."

"Lead the way," Fargo said, and let himself be led through the doorway. He twisted to call to Caleb, "I'll be down to relieve you as soon as I can."

"No hurry," the skinny Shaker replied.

The cool interior of the dwellings felt almost as good as a cold shower after the ordeal Fargo had been through. He noticed that Gretchen wasn't taking the same route Chilton had showed him the night before. When she came to one of the rooms, she took a left instead of going straight and went through two more doorways, then turned to the right.

"Hey, where are you taking me?" he asked, sliding the tomahawk under his belt.

They had just entered a small room. A window high on the front wall filtered shafts of dusty, subdued light onto the center of the floor.

Gretchen halted and stepped in front of Fargo, her bosom nearly touching his chest. Her upturned, radiant face was exquisitely attractive. "I was hoping you would give me a little of your time."

"For what?" Fargo asked, knowing the answer before he opened his mouth.

"You know," Gretchen said huskily, then stood on tiptoe to plant her soft, moist lips on his own. It was more a peck than a kiss, and she quickly bowed her head as if ashamed of her own boldness.

Fargo cleared his throat. She was a pretty filly, undeniably. Any man in his right mind would gladly jump into bed with her. But although she possessed the body of a woman, emotionally she was very much like a child and had no idea what she was in for. "Aren't you rushing it a bit?" he asked.

Her head came up, her eyes defiant. "Not at all. The way I see it, I've already wasted too much of my life as it is. And I don't want to waste another minute. Tomorrow I might be dead, for all I know." She stroked his cheek, and her next words were uttered haltingly. "I don't want to die not knowing. I've never even really kissed a man."

"Never?" Fargo asked, certain he must have misunderstood.

"Not once."

"Well, I'll be."

"Now do you understand?"

"I reckon I do," Fargo said. He admired her forthright courage. How many women would go after their first sexual experience so aggressively?

"Please."

The eloquent appeal in her eyes moved Fargo in more ways than one. He leaned forward and gently kissed her lips, her chin, and her soft throat. She stood stone still, her eyes wide, her cherry lips slightly parted, her sweet breath issuing in excited spurts.

"That sort of tickles," Gretchen said nervously when he straightened.

"It's not too late to back out," Fargo said, giving her a last chance before she got him fully aroused. Already his manhood was at half-mast.

Gretchen didn't flinch. "I want to know."

Placing both hands on her slim shoulders, Fargo kissed her again, this time parting her lips with his tongue so he could probe the silken depths of her mouth. Gretchen hesitantly touched her tongue to his. He lowered his hands to her breasts. Although not as large as her sister's, they stood out against the fabric with firm youthfulness. She cooed deep in her throat as he caressed them, his thumbs pressing on her prominent nipples. Their kiss went on and on, stoking Gretchen's inner fire, and she hungrily sucked on his tongue while grinding her hips against his.

Fargo felt light-headed. Whether it was from passion, a lack of food, or a reaction to all the excitement earlier, he couldn't tell. His right hand traced a path down her flat belly to the junction of her thighs, and his fingers felt the heat emanating from between her legs. With his palm he massaged her mound and she squirmed delightfully.

His organ had reached its full length. Now it pulsated, eager for release, but he wasn't about to rush. Since this was Gretchen's first time, he wanted to make it an experience she would recollect fondly. So he rubbed her breasts and her mound until she sagged against him and panted heavily in his ear.

"Oh, my," she said.

He began stripping off his shirt and she helped him, running her hands over his hard-muscled chest when the garment fell at their feet. Her hands never stopped moving. She seemed to be trying to drink him in through her palms. Bringing his right hand up, he threw aside her shawl and worked at unbuttoning her dress. Gretchen took small breaths and closed her eyes.

Fargo felt her tense when he finally unfastened the dress completely and it dropped to the floor around her slender ankles. Her undergarments posed the next obstacle, and he removed them slowly, delicately, savoring the sight of her beautiful naked body as her pale skin was gradually exposed to his view. When at last she stood without a stitch of clothing on, he licked her neck and bent down to fasten his mouth to her pert left breast. His tongue flicked its pink tip and she arched her spine.

"Ooooooh. Oh, yes."

He transferred his attention to her other breast, enjoying the way it swelled under his manipulation, while simultaneously pulling off his boots and pants. He nearly lost his balance, but soon his clothes were beside hers. She put her hands on his chest and pushed back, and he thought she might have changed her mind at the last moment. Instead, she brazenly studied his physique from head to toe.

Fargo said nothing. He let her set the pace.

"How can it fit?" Gretchen asked.

"We'll take it slow at first," he said.

Licking her lips, Gretchen reached out and wrapped her right hand around his long pole. "Oh," she said, and lightly stroked it from top to bottom.

Shuddering in ecstasy, Fargo felt his manhood tingle. He reined in his fiery desire, not wanting to spoil it for her.

"Does that feel nice?" Gretchen naively inquired.

"You don't know the half of it," Fargo said, closing his eyes. He nearly jumped when her mouth replaced her hand and her lips nibbled at his organ as if at an ear of corn. He smoothed her hair, his mouth abruptly dry. Lord, she was good. Give her a few years and the lucky man she married would be set for life. She dallied down there for a long time, her carnal thirst unquenchable now that it had been aroused.

Finally he pulled her up and locked his lips on hers, his hands again moving over her breasts. Her hips were flush with his, his organ tight against her mound, her downy hairs cushioning his shaft.

Fargo eased her to the dusty floor, her bottom on his buckskins, and knelt between her legs. She looked up at him in questioning wonder, then gasped when he lowered his face to her crack and darted his tongue into her moist womanhood. The gasp became an animal moan when he licked her in earnest, and her thighs involuntarily constricted on his head.

"Yes, yes. Oh, yes. Go on. Please."

He ate her, lapping at her until her body bucked and thrashed, his tongue touching her knob again and again. Her hands in his hair, she swung her head from side to side, the tip of her tongue protruding, her passion mounting to an uncontrollable summit. When his face was slick with her juices, and his tongue tired from his ministrations, he rose onto his knees once more and carefully inserted the tip of his organ into her hole.

Gretchen tensed and gazed at him almost fearfully.

He knew she was afraid it would hurt. If he was too rough now, he might sour her on men forever. Tenderly, he slid his manhood in a fraction at a time, her slick inner walls wrapping around him like a glove. There was no obstruction, although her tunnel narrowed at the top and he had to give a slight shove to bury himself to the hilt.

"Dear Lord!" Gretchen whispered, her nostrils flaring.

Fargo commenced pumping, using leisurely movements, and her body responded superbly, meeting every thrust with a counterthrust, nature taking its course. Their lips met and his fingers squeezed her pliant breasts. He didn't know how long it would take her to go over the edge, but he was committed to giving her the ultimate pleasure before he allowed himself to explode. To his surprise she suddenly went into a frenzy, her body bouncing wildly, her nails digging into his back as she bit him on the shoulder. Her juices enveloped his manhood and he saw her eyelids flutter.

"Ahhhhh! Oh! This is heaven!"

He held himself still until her heaving subsided and she lay under him, spent and languorous. She licked her lips, smiled wanly, and kissed the tip of his jaw.

"Thank you. That was wonderful."

"We're not done yet."

"What?" Gretchen said, and then felt him still inside. Her eyes widened. "Oh, God," she said.

Smiling, Fargo began stroking again, not holding back this time.

"Oh, *God!*"

11

"Where have the two of you been?" Sister Naomi inquired when Fargo and Gretchen walked into the dwelling that housed the women an hour later. "We wanted to hold a meeting, but you were nowhere around."

"I gave Skye a tour," Gretchen answered, using the fib the two of them had agreed upon earlier when she had expressed concern about how her brethren would react to her absence.

Fargo nodded. "I wanted to make sure there was no way for the Navahos to get up here without us knowing about it." He paused, scanning the others in the room. "I didn't count on it taking so long."

None of the Shakers present—Naomi, Ruth, Thomas, or Chilton—seemed disposed to doubt the story. They were inherently trusting souls and accepted statements at their face value. It would never occur to them, Fargo reflected, that Gretchen or he would lie.

"We're safe unless the savages build new ladders to scale the lower walls," Chilton said. "But there isn't enough wood in the surrounding countryside to make a stool, let alone a long ladder."

"The ones we left down there will fall apart if those Indians try to use them," Thomas added, not quite able to suppress a trace of a malicious grin at the idea of the Navahos injuring themselves in the attempt.

"I noticed," Fargo said, and saw their water bag lying in a corner, its sides almost totally flat. He walked over and picked it up. "This needs to be refilled."

"We know," Chilton said. "I was bringing water back from the spring last night when we tangled, remember? I threw all of it in your face. No one has been able to sneak off since."

"I'll go now," Fargo offered. "Tell me where to find this spring."

"I'd have to show you," Chilton said.

Naomi looked at both of them. "Shouldn't you wait until tonight, when there is less chance of being spotted by the Navahos?"

Fargo hefted the limp leather bag. "After the licking they took, they might not be back for a spell." He hefted the bag and stepped to the doorway. "I'm thirsty enough to drink all of this in two gulps, which would leave us with none for the rest of the day. In ten minutes I can be back with a full bag and we can all drink as much as we want."

"You're taking the bag with you?" Chilton asked.

"I can't carry the water back in my pockets," Fargo answered.

"I've always taken our bucket," Chilton said. "That way, if the Navahos were to catch me, the rest would still have the water bag and could go after more whenever they want."

"One bucketful of water won't fill this bag," Fargo said. "You must need to make several trips."

"Four or five," Chilton admitted.

"Giving the Navahos that many more chances to nab you," Fargo said. "We'll take the bag. Come on."

"Hold on a minute. There's something you're forgetting," Chilton said, and hurried out in the direction of the quarters where the men slept.

"How about our meeting?" Naomi asked. "We need to discuss what happened to Sister Joan and Brother Paul."

"What is there to talk about?" Fargo said. "They're both dead, and all of us will soon be too unless we find a way out of here."

"We can make a go of it," Naomi said, her tone lacking conviction.

"You can keep on fooling yourself right into the grave for all I care," Fargo said. "But I'm leaving the first chance I get, and I'm taking anyone who wants to go with me."

"I'll go," Gretchen interjected.

"So will Caleb and Chilton," Fargo predicted, giving Naomi, Ruth, and Thomas long stares. "And if you folks have any brains, you'll go with us." An uncomfortable silence descended as the Shakers mulled over his words. He was pleased to see doubt etching the faces of the three holdouts. It meant they could be persuaded to let common sense prevail. Apparently only Joan and Paul had possessed the same unshakable conviction as the sect's late misguided leader.

Chilton came back bearing a rope looped over his left shoulder. "Now we're all set," he said.

Fargo led the way down to the lowest level, where they found Caleb pacing back and forth on the same terrace, the rifle held loosely in the crook of his arm.

"Off for water, eh?" he said, his eyes on the water bag, and stifled a yawn. His features drooped in fatigue.

"Yep," Fargo responded. "And as soon as we get back, I'm pulling guard duty."

"I recall hearing that offer before," Caleb said, grinning.

"I mean it this time," Fargo promised, and stepped to the rim. The rope lay at the bottom. There was no sign of the war party anywhere in the vast cavern. "Have you seen anything of the Navahos?" he asked.

"It's been quiet since they rode off," Caleb reported. "Maybe they've learned their lesson."

"I wouldn't count on it," Fargo said, and took the rope from Chilton. He tied it securely, tossing the coils over the side, and tucked the water bag under his right arm. In no time he was standing at the base of the wall, the tomahawk in his left hand, waiting for the Shaker to join him.

Chilton, his speed retarded by his clipped wing, slid slowly to the bottom. "That didn't hurt half as bad as I figured it would," he said. "My arm will be as good as new in a few days."

"Which way?" Fargo asked, not inclined to make small talk when the Navahos might come back at any moment.

Motioning with his left arm, Chilton jogged toward the rear of the cavern, staying close to the wall.

"How did you find this spring?" Fargo inquired.

"By a fluke," Chilton answered. "I was searching for another way out of the cavern, poking my head into every crack and cranny I found, when I came on a narrow opening. Smelled the water right off. We've been using it ever since.'' His voice lowered. ''Brother Paul claimed the Lord put it there for our salvation.''

Fargo gazed far overhead and discovered a fluttering mass of small black creatures hanging upside down from the ceiling. His skin did some fluttering of its own. ''Bats,'' he muttered.

''Thousands of them,'' Chilton said. ''During the day they're so quiet you hardly know they are up there. About sundown, though, they begin squealing and flapping their wings. Then they all fly out. Spoky thing to see, I tell you.'' He looked up and licked his lips. ''They don't show up again until almost dawn.''

Suddenly Fargo's boots started making squishing noises and he glanced down, revulsion sweeping through him as he realized he was walking in a four-or-five-inch-deep layer of bat droppings that covered the ground for dozens of square yards. A disgusting odor made him want to gag.

Chilton didn't seem to mind. He was following the angle of the lower wall as it gradually curved toward the cavern wall behind the cliff dwellings.

Minutes later, well clear of the bat droppings, they were at the base of the shadow-shrouded cavern wall. Towering to their right were the ancient buildings. To their left were the murky recesses of the cavern. At such a distance from the entrance, the sunlight was feeble at best.

''This way,'' Chilton said, moving to the left.

The cavern wall was marred by scores of cracks and wider clefts. Fargo understood why the Shaker would have had a hard time explaining which one was the right one. Underfoot, dust swirled into the air with every stride he took. Other than the Shakers, whose tracks were plain to see, no one had been in that corner of the cavern in ages. He couldn't see the front opening from where they were, which was reassuring because it meant the Navahos couldn't see them, either.

''Not far now,'' Chilton stated, slowing and studying the dark stone wall intently. ''Sometimes I go right past it.''

Fargo was passing a cleft a yard wide. A faint whisper of warm air stroked his right cheek and he halted in surprise, then turned. Could it be? ''Hold up,'' he said, and stepped up to the cleft to poke his head inside. The air was warmer still.

"What are you doing, friend? This isn't where the spring is located."

"Stand here," Fargo directed, moving aside.

"I don't under—" Chilton began, then stiffened as he faced into the opening. "I'll be. This is air from the outside."

"My thinking exactly. Have you explored this cleft?"

"No," Chilton said, and thoughtfully rubbed under his chin. "Why didn't I notice the warm air before?"

"Maybe the breeze wasn't as strong then, or the wind outside was blowing from another direction," Fargo speculated. "Show me the spring; then we'll check to see if we're right."

"If it's wide enough we can escape the Navahos," Chilton said excitedly.

"Don't get your hopes up yet," Fargo cautioned.

The Shaker went on, and twenty feet farther halted beside a dark opening half as wide as the previous cleft. The sides narrowed near the bottom and formed a solid stone barrier for the final two feet. "Reach inside," Chilton said.

Fargo scented the tantalizing odor of the water immediately. He stuck the tomahawk handle under his belt, bent over, and extended his arm. The barrier, he found, was actually the outer rim of a large stone bowl filled with cool water. His arm sank in up to the elbow. Cupping his hand, he raised the liquid to his lips and took a swallow. Unlike the water at Adobe Wells, this was pure and delicious.

"I wonder if the people who once lived here knew about this spring," Chilton commented idly.

"Most likely," Fargo said. Opening the bag, he held it under the surface and listened to the air bubbles that agitated the water. At first the sound of the bubbles was continuous; as the bag filled, it lessened. When the bubbling ceased, he lifted the now heavy waterskin and replaced the stopper. Then he hurried to the cleft where the warm air originated.

"Want me to fetch a torch?" Chilton asked.

"Just hold this," Fargo said, and handed over the bag. "Stay here and warn me if the Navahos show up."

"Will do."

Turning sideways, Fargo pulled out the tomahawk again and

eased into the cleft. Holding the weapon by the head and using the handle as a blind man would use a cane, he poked and prodded while cautiously advancing into the murky interior. The sides closed in until there were mere inches to spare and the ceiling lowered to just above his head. His main worry was falling into a pit or a deep crevasse, so he placed his foot down lightly each time, coiled to hurl himself backward should his sole contact empty air.

The passageway went straight for thirty or forty feet, then slanted to the right and climbed upward.

Fargo scraped his head and had to hunch over in order to keep going. Total blackness engulfed him, giving him a creepy feeling. Unreasoning panic gnawed at his mind, but he shrugged it off. Once he heard a faint scraping, as if a tiny creature had dashed or slithered past in front of him, and his skin crawled worse than it had when he saw the bats.

He lost precise track of the distance and the time. After three minutes—or was it five?—the pervading darkness seemed to lighten somewhat. Suddenly his left boot smacked into something that rattled, and he halted. Leaning over, he felt with his fingers until they contacted a pile of smooth, slender objects partially covered by the dust of ages. He picked one up and ran his hands over it, trying to figure out what it was. The ends were wider than the long center portion and were capped by rounded knobs. The shape disturbed him. He felt he should know what it was, and as he lowered his arm to release it, insight dawned.

A bone!

He let it go and wiped his hands on his buckskins, taking turns with each palm so he could switch the tomahawk from one hand to the other. From the size and shape, he knew it had been a leg bone, a human leg bone, and his mouth went dry with misgiving. From the number of bones he'd touched, he deduced an entire skeleton lay at his feet. What was it doing there? Had one of the Indians who long ago occupied the cliff town perished at that very spot?

Fargo gingerly elevated his right foot to step over the bones but accidentally bumped them. His heel came down on a large round object, which he figured must be the skull, and he almost slipped. Girding himself, he pressed deeper into the passage.

To his relief, the ceiling rose higher and the walls became farther apart. He could stand upright once more and walk normally. Even better, he could see almost a few inches in front of his face. Gaining confidence and eager to reach the end, he moved faster.

The breeze became stronger and hotter. Sweat broke out on his brow and he wished he'd brought the water bag along. His right shoulder smacked into the wall, making him wince, and he stopped. By tapping with the tomahawk handle, he determined that the passage turned to the left.

Fargo rubbed his shoulder and carefully walked around the corner. Stretching out both hands and keeping them in front of his head so he would know if the passageway changed direction again, he strode up an incline. Far ahead he spotted a glimmer of light, and smiled. He'd done it! With any luck, he'd be able to report back to the others that he'd found a way out. They'd pack up and leave by morning, and—

Fargo's train of thought was abruptly derailed when his legs shot out from under him and he plummeted into an inky void.

12

In the very instant that his feet plunged into emptiness and a blast of cool air struck his face, Fargo let go of the tomahawk and twisted around sharply, throwing his arms out behind him. He hit the rim of the Stygian abyss hard, wrenching both arms from the shoulders to the wrists, and caught desperate hold of the grainy earth, his body and legs suspended below, mere heartbeats away from slipping into eternity. His arms immediately began to slide lower, and he dug in his fingernails with fierce determination, sinking them into the soil to arrest his fall.

For a few moments Fargo had a breather. He clung there, gathering his breath and his wits, and inched his legs back and forth, striving to find a purchase for his feet. There was none. Then, from far below, came the dull thud of the tomahawk striking the bottom of the chasm. The drop, he reckoned, must be a hundred feet or more. If he lost his grip, he was doomed.

Gritting his teeth, Fargo tried to pull himself up. His arms ached terribly, but he got both shoulders above the rim. His chin scraped the musty ground and dust swirled into his nose, which promptly tingled as if he'd inhaled pepper. He knew he was about to sneeze and dreaded the possible consequences if doing so should cause him to lose his grip. His nose scrunched up and he opened his mouth, his head involuntarily whipping back. With a sudden motion he lowered his face to the edge, jamming his nose against the earth and pressing it shut. The tingling stopped and the urge to sneeze gradually passed.

He lifted his head and redoubled his efforts to climb out, gouging his knees and toes into the side of the chasm. His fingers became rigid claws. His breath came in ragged gasps. And slowly, ever so slowly, he pulled himself up until the upper third of his chest was above the edge and he was supported on his elbows.

He paused again for a brief rest, and glanced over his right shoulder. The distant glimmer of light still beckoned, but it might as well be on another continent for all the good it would do him and the Shakers. Wriggling his torso, he snaked all the way out, then crawled another yard for safety's sake. His left hand bumped a small rock and he picked it up before cautiously standing.

Glad at having solid ground under his feet again, he faced the chasm, transferred the rock to his right hand, and executed an underhand throw, tossing the rock as high as he could to give it a longer trajectory. A second elapsed. Two. Finally the rock landed on the opposite side with a distinct thud.

Disappointed, Fargo began retracing his steps. The chasm was too wide to jump. He must find another way out of the cavern soon, before the Shakers ran out of food or more Navahos showed up. Checking every cleft in the cavern was out of the question. Not only would it take too long, but as he had just learned, it would also be too dangerous.

Chilton was waiting anxiously when Fargo at last appeared and eased out of the opening. "Praise the Lord, friend. I was beginning to think we'd lost you."

"You almost did," Fargo said, and took the water bag. "Any trouble while I was gone?"

"It's been as quiet as a tomb."

Poor choice of words, Fargo reflected, thinking of his near scrape with death. He took the lead, hustling along the wall, past the bats, and to the terrace where Caleb waited.

"All clear," the Shaker called down. "Those red devils haven't shown their faces yet."

Fargo knelt and tied the end of the rope around the top of the water bag. "Haul away," he said, and stood as the rope jerked upward.

Chilton was examining his bandaged arm.

"Maybe you shouldn't have tagged along," Fargo commented. "Are you up to the climb?"

"Don't worry about me," Chilton responded. "Staying down here to have my throat slit when those red heathens come back doesn't particularly appeal to me. My arm is sore, but I'll make it okay."

And he did. After Caleb lowered the rope, Chilton scaled it easily.

Fargo went last. Once on top he held out his hand for the rifle, which Caleb handed over without any objection.

"I'm tuckered out," the skinny Shaker said. "Figure I'll saw logs for ten hours, at least."

"Before you do, I want to call a meeting," Fargo said. "I know how tired you are, but it's important."

"Where and when?" Caleb asked.

"Right here and now."

"I'll get the others," Caleb said, and departed with the water bag.

"Why not hold the meeting higher up?" Chilton asked.

"I can see the cavern entrance better from here," Fargo said, and sank onto one knee, his attention shifting to the dark mass of slumbering bats. "You say those critters fly out every day after sundown?"

"Like clockwork," Chilton said.

"How long does it take all of them to leave?"

"I never timed it, but I'd guess three or four minutes, thereabouts. Why?"

Fargo glanced at the entrance. Thousands of bats swarming out at once wouldn't leave much room for anything else to try to leave, but it was still their best bet. "I have an idea," he told Chilton, and said nothing else until Caleb and the rest arrived.

"What's this about *you* calling a meeting?" Naomi promptly demanded.

"I'll get straight to the point," Fargo said, rising. "We're all leaving at sundown."

The Shakers exchanged surprised glances.

"So soon?" Thomas asked.

"Why not wait a day?" Ruth inquired.

"How much jerky do you have left?" Fargo rejoined.

"None," Ruth said.

"Now you know why we can't wait."

"But we can hunt for lizards and such," Naomi said. "We've caught a few before."

"Do you aim to eat lizard the rest of your life?" Fargo snapped.

Naomi didn't answer.

"I'm not going to waste my breath arguing with you folks," Fargo declared. "We're out of food. Every day we delay will make us that much weaker. We must leave today, while we're still in good shape, or we'll never be able to cross the Jornada del Muerto."

"But we haven't quite made up our minds whether we want to leave or not," Naomi said. "We must put the issue to a vote and act accordingly."

"No vote," Fargo said.

Naomi recoiled in shock. "I beg your pardon. Who do you think you are to tell us what to do?"

Fargo had reached the limits of his patience. "I'll tell you who I am," he growled, taking a menacing step toward her. "I'm the one hope you have of getting out of this fix alive. And I'm leaving at sunset. So unless you want to share the same fate as Joan, Paul, and the rest of your brethren, you'd be smart to get your tail back up there and try to rest before we leave."

"You can count me in," Caleb said.

"Me too," Gretchen stated.

Chilton simply nodded.

The youngest, Thomas, turned uncertain eyes on Naomi and Ruth, then looked at the other men. "I agree it's time to leave, but I won't if they don't."

"Do you hear that?" Fargo addressed Naomi. "He's green enough to stick with you if you decide to stay, and his death will be on your conscience for as long as you live, which won't be long." He saw her grimace, saw her avert her gaze, and knew he'd won even before he heard her sigh of resignation.

"All right. We'll all go with you."

Praise the Lord! Fargo wanted to say, but didn't. He pointed at the bats. "At sundown those things leave. I want everyone ready by then. We'll take the water bag, any knives you have, and this rifle."

"That's all?" Naomi asked. "What about blankets to cover

ourselves at night? And we have cooking utensils that would come in handy.''

"We'll be traveling at night," Fargo informed her. "If we catch any lizards or snakes, we'll eat them raw." He paused and raked them with a hard stare. "The more we carry, the thirstier we get, so we'll go light. Make no mistake. This will be the hardest thing any of you have ever done, but if we ration the water, and if we're damned lucky, we'll get out of it alive.''

None of them spoke.

Fargo gestured at the doorway. "Off you go. I'll keep guard until it's time to leave." He watched them obey, all except Gretchen, who stayed put, her arms crossed, grinning impishly. "Didn't you hear me?"

She strolled up to him until their bodies were nearly touching. "It's still early. I thought we might pay our private room another visit.''

"Didn't you just hear me? I have to keep guard until we leave.''

Gretchen smiled again and traced a fingertip along his chin. "What harm would it do if you slipped away for half an hour?''

"Plenty, if the Navahos came back while I was gone.''

"They can't get up here. The others will be fine.''

Fargo shook his head in amazement. It never failed. Take any female, even the most inexperienced or frigid woman around, and once her sexual appetite was fully aroused she became insatiable. For all the general talk and joking about how men never got enough, there were times when he believed women were more aggressive in sexual affairs than men. And here was Gretchen proving his point all over again. "I can't," he said. "Sorry. But our safety comes first.''

"You didn't find me pleasing," she said, pouting.

"Believe me, I've never met a woman more pleasing," Fargo assured her. "But I really can't leave.''

Frowning, Gretchen wheeled and strode away. "It's your loss, Mr. Fargo," she said formally. "I hope you don't regret your decision later.''

Recalling her silken thighs and hot kisses, Fargo also frowned. "I'm already regretting it," he mumbled, and faced the cavern floor. He had a long wait until sunset. Moving to the rim, he sat down and swung his legs over the side. What was he letting himself in for? he mused. The Shakers were the last folks he'd care to cross a desert with. Total greenhorns, they were bound to cause him untold grief. Which, considering how wonderfully everything had gone since he'd left Albuquerque, wouldn't change his run of luck one bit.

By Fargo's inner clock it was an hour or so shy of sundown when he led the Shakers from the cliff dwellings toward the cavern mouth. They walked in single file, sticking near the wall, each one a study in nervousness, even Caleb and Chilton. Young Thomas carried the water bag. Since the rifle belonged to Caleb, Fargo had offered to give it back to him, but the lean Shaker politely refused to take it, and then handed over an ammunition pouch and a powder horn. When Fargo had asked why, he received a straightforward answer.

"I imagine you're a better shot than I am, and once we're out there every shot will count."

Now Fargo hefted the weapon and apprehensively regarded the entrance. If the Navahos should appear while the Shakers were far from cover, he'd be hard-pressed to save them. The same would hold true once they were crossing the desert, but he couldn't let himself dwell on the worst that could happen. And the way he saw it, he'd rather go down fighting than suffer an agonizing slow death from starvation.

He reached the cavern mouth and halted, then motioned for the others to stand with their backs to the stone wall. The next step was up to the bats. He was amazed the furry things hadn't flown off during the battle earlier, when the rifle was booming and the Navahos were whooping. Snug in their high roost, they hadn't been in the least disturbed by the human activity below.

Once, on a sunny afternoon years ago, he'd watched two boys do some bat hunting at a farmhouse. The bats, he'd been told, slept behind the shutters during the day, then flew out at night to catch insects. Armed with crude clubs they had fashioned from broken tree limbs, the boys had gone from shutter to shutter and attempted to drive the bats into the open by pounding on the slats. Not one bat had emerged until the boys took to throwing the shutters closed. Five or six had been beaten to a pulp before they could climb into the air.

Fargo looked at the Shakers. He'd explained his plan before climbing down from the terrace, but a reminder wouldn't hurt. "We wait until the bats fly out of the cavern," he reiterated. "As the last ones go by, run as fast as you can to the nearest boulders."

"What if the Navahos are out there?" Thomas asked.

"They must know the bats leave every day at the same time," Fargo said. "So they won't pay much attention. If we time it right, the bats will hide us from them until we're almost to those boulders."

"I pray you're right, friend," Thomas said.

That makes two of us, Fargo thought, gazing at the winged multitude. He passed the time impatiently, regretting he'd brought the Shakers to the entrance so early. But he couldn't risk the bats departing sooner than they ordinarily did and ruining his whole plan. He fidgeted, shifting his weight from foot to foot. The sunlight streaming into the cavern dimmed gradually as twilight fell.

He was leaning against the wall, the rifle cradled in his arms, when loud squeals and rapid flapping issued from the roof. Looking up, he beheld the bats in the act of rousing themselves, many stretching their leathery wings and flapping them in preparation for flight. This activity continued for a while, and then a single large bat swooped toward the entrance and the rest instantly followed suit, forming a roiling cloud of pointed ears, brown fur, and tapered teeth that bore down on Fargo like demonic creatures out of his worst nightmare.

13

In a tremendous rush of flapping wings, the bat horde reached the mouth of the cavern.

Fargo pressed his back against the wall and instinctively elevated his arms to protect his face, even though none of the creatures tried to attack him. They were close, however, so close he could reach out and touch them if he wanted. An awful, pungent odor assailed his nostrils, and he breathed shallowly to keep from inhaling it.

The winged multitude filled the entrance from top to bottom and from one side to the other. Despite being packed together, they flew with flawless precision, and once they were clear of the cavern they arched up into the darkening sky in a steady stream of furry forms.

A continuous gust of fetid air fanned by their combined flapping movements struck Fargo on the face. Dust rose from the cavern floor. He blinked, concentrating on the cloud of bats, aware the timing was critical. It seemed to take forever for all the bats to depart on their nocturnal rounds, but at last he saw the end of the cloud and shouted so the others would be ready. "Here we go! Stay close to me."

The very moment that the final fringe of bats reached the entrance, Fargo broke into a run and sprinted out of the cavern in their wake. In front of him rose a wide column of the critters stretching far up into the heavens. He slanted to the left, staying low, moving as fast as he could, scouring the boulders for the Navahos.

To the west the sun had disappeared below the horizon.

Fargo looked back once to verify that the Shakers were following. Gretchen was right behind him, then came Chilton, Naomi, Thomas, Ruth, and Caleb. He slowed as he neared the first huge boulder, and crouched at its base until they caught up.

"We did it!" Ruth whispered.

"Break out the whiskey, why don't you?" Fargo said dryly, and moved stealthily around the boulder.

"But none of us drink," Ruth replied.

Some folks, Fargo reflected, were hopeless cases before they were even born. He gazed up at the blossoming stars. The Big Dipper was visible, and he had no difficulty in finding the North Star. He adjusted his course accordingly, making for Adobe Wells.

"Where do you think the Navahos are?" Gretchen inquired softly.

"I don't know and I don't rightly care so long as it's not anywhere near us," Fargo answered. "Now pipe down, all of you, and keep your eyes peeled." He led them around the mesa, using every boulder and gully for cover, until they reached a flat stretch that extended northward as far as he could see. Now came the truly perilous part.

Motioning with his right arm, Fargo headed into the heart of the desert. He didn't bother to look back at the mesa. If he never saw it again, it would be too soon. Fortunately the temperature had dropped a bit since the sun went down and would fall even more in the next couple of hours. A slow, cool breeze from the northwest added to the comfortable conditions, a far cry from the inferno that would exist after dawn.

He hiked tirelessly on, gazing at the Shakers every so often to see if any were having trouble keeping up. They held their own marvelously, giving him no cause to complain, until approximately four hours after their departure.

Fargo called a halt on the rim of an oval depression over four feet deep and twenty feet in diameter. He jumped down, then turned to assist the women. Once everyone was seated, he told Thomas to give everyone a drink. To his annoyance, the Shaker proceeded to open the water bag and take deep gulps. In three strides Fargo was next to him, yanking the water bag out of his hands. "What the hell do you think you're doing?" he demanded.

The youth gaped. "What's wrong? You said we could have some."

"I didn't mean for you to drink it all at once," Fargo said.

"This water has to last us until we reach Adobe Wells. Take small sips, don't guzzle it."

Thomas lowered his head. "Sorry, friend. I guess I wasn't thinking."

Fargo took the bag to Gretchen, let her take several sips, and then went from Shaker to Shaker until all of them had lessened their thirst. He brought the precious bag back to Thomas. "Here. I'll give you a second chance."

"Thank you," the young man said, taking it.

Little else was said during the brief rest. The Shakers stared at the surrounding desert as if seeing it for the first time, impressed by the enormity of the Jornada del Muerto and the daunting feat they were attempting.

Fargo gave the order to continue and took the lead once again. Every so often a coyote would yip, always off in the distance. Another mesa materialized in their path, and they neared its base an hour later. Squatter than the mesa containing the cavern, its sides were nevertheless equally as steep and impossible to climb. He hiked along its base, in gloom compounded by a total, ominous silence, and was glad when they left the mesa behind to strike off across another stretch of barren desert.

By Fargo's reckoning it was past three in the morning when he heard a faint yell to their rear and drew up short, pivoting to listen for a second one.

Each Shaker likewise halted.

"What was that?" Gretchen asked.

"Navaho, most likely," Fargo said.

"Why was he yelling?"

"Could have been a signal."

Another yell emphasized Fargo's notion.

"Do you mean they're signaling back and forth to one another?" Chilton asked.

"That'd be my hunch."

"Do you think they're on our trail?"

"I know they are," Fargo said. "They're tracking us, which isn't very easy to do at night. But they've likely figured out that we're heading for Adobe Wells, so they can make a beeline due north and not worry too much about losing the sign."

Naomi brushed at her bangs and nervously asked, "How long before they catch us?"

"No way of telling yet," Fargo said, moving out.

The Shakers whispered excitedly among themselves, agitated by the knowledge the Navahos were after them.

"It won't do no good to get yourselves worked up," Fargo said without turning. "Save your breath for walking. We need to find a spot to make our stand and do it pronto."

"Stand?" Gretchen repeated.

"The place where we'll ambush the Navahos," Fargo elaborated. Off to the right he spotted several saguaros, resembling a string of fence posts. Where there were a few there might be many more, and if so the Navahos were in for a big surprise.

He walked silently while the Shakers constantly made noise by accidentally kicking stones or clumping through occasional patches of sagebrush. Criticizing them would do little good. They lacked his skill and were doing the best they could. Still, when one of them stepped on a dry twig as they were passing a stunted mesquite tree, he said, "Try not to advertise our whereabouts if you can help it."

More saguaros appeared. As was often the case, they tended to appear in large numbers where the soil was conducive to their growth, forming a virtual forest of silent sentinels with their many prickly arms upturned to the heavens.

Fargo advanced for scores of yards before he halted and surveyed the saguaros around them. Many grew in clusters that were ideal hiding places. "This is it," he announced.

"What?" Naomi asked.

"Where we'll make our stand," Fargo said, and indicated the encircling cactuses. "The women will—"

"Is this really necessary?" Naomi inquired, stepping forward. "If we keep going we might be able to elude the Navahos."

"They're on horseback. We're on foot," Fargo explained as if to a four-year-old. "They'll overtake us soon. If we can give them a scare and kill one or two in the bargain, they'll skedaddle and leave us alone for a spell."

"Some of us might die," Naomi said.

"All of us will die unless we fight back," Fargo stated. "Now take Ruth and Gretchen and find a spot to hide about twenty yards from where I'm standing. Lay low and don't speak until it's all over.''

''What if they kill all of you?''

''Then offer yourself to the first buck who finds you and maybe he'll take you into his lodge as one of his wives,'' Fargo said with a straight face.

''I suppose you think your horrible suggestion is funny?'' Naomi retorted.

''It wasn't a joke,'' Fargo said. ''Navahos sometimes take white women captive. They don't rate our womenfolk very high as wifely material, but sometimes one of them will take a real fancy to a pretty gal and treat her decent.''

''I refuse to become the wife of one of those heathens. I'd rather die.''

''Then your problem is solved,'' Fargo said, taking her by the arm and propelling her gently to the east. ''Now do as I told you and be quick about it. And take the water bag.''

Naomi complied, her spine stiff in resentment, and the three women hastened into the saguaros.

''What about us?'' Caleb asked. ''You have the only gun. All we have to fight with are knives and our fists.''

''You can count me out,'' young Thomas said. ''I will not strike another living soul in anger.''

Fargo looked at him. ''Who says you have to attack them in anger? Hell, you can stab them with love in your heart and a smile on your face if it will make you happy. But we can use your help.''

''No,'' Thomas said. ''It's against my religious convictions. I'm a Shaker, after all, and I haven't forsaken my vows like these two did.'' He nodded at Caleb and Chilton.

''I don't have time to argue,'' Fargo said. ''Go hide with the ladies if you want.''

The youth hurried after them.

''Can the three of us do it by ourselves?'' Chilton inquired.

''We don't have much choice, do we?'' Fargo rejoined bitterly, and walked to a tall cactus on the right. ''Caleb, you lie behind this saguaro and don't show yourself unless one of the warriors rides close enough for you to reach him in one jump. Then stab him so many times he'll bleed like a sieve."

"I'll do my best," the skinny Shaker promised, and flattened, holding a knife in his right hand.

Fargo glanced at Chilton. "Now for you." He moved to a cactus twenty feet to the left of the one shielding Caleb. "This is your spot. The same goes for you. Don't make your move unless you're damn sure you can get one of them before he gets you. I don't want to lose anyone."

Chilton hesitated. "There's something you should know."

"What?"

"I've never killed anyone before. I've struck the Navahos, but I didn't take a life."

"Do you think you can?"

"I honestly can't say."

Fargo gazed along their back trail. The Navahos might appear at any moment and he had to be in position. "If you want to join the women, go ahead."

"I'd like to be of some assistance to you," Chilton said, and bit his lower lip. "I wouldn't feel right doing nothing."

The man's obvious inner conflict got Fargo to thinking. He wasn't a particularly religious hombre himself, but he wasn't necessarily irreligious either. He figured every person had a right to believe whatever they wanted and no one should try to impose their views on anyone else. So he couldn't force the Shaker to do something that went against the man's grain. "I won't hold it against you if you don't care to fight," he said softly.

Chilton unexpectedly dropped down behind the cactus. "I'll do what I can, but I'm not making any promises."

"Fair enough," Fargo said, and moved eastward a dozen yards. His plan was simple. He'd let the Navahos go past him, then blast one off his horse. The rest would turn toward him, putting their backs to the two Shakers and enabling Caleb and Chilton to jump them unseen.

There were four saguaros standing in a small square, and he stepped into the center and squatted. He had a clear view of the desert, and it was unlikely the warriors would spot him if he hunkered low to the ground. Now all he had to do was wait.

The night seemed unnaturally quiet. Not even a cricket chirped.

He placed his thumb on the hammer of the rifle, his mind straying. Grace Davenport was definitely getting her money's worth. Two thousand dollars was a paltry sum in light of the hardships he'd encountered so far and would soon encounter again. The next time he accepted such a job, he'd know enough to ask for double the amount.

The next time?

He grinned at his foolishness. If he ever pulled such a hair-brained stunt again—pretty woman or no pretty woman—he deserved to be strung up by his thumbs over burning coals.

Something moved out on the desert.

Easing lower, Fargo held his breath and felt his heart pound in his chest. Spectral riders appeared. Two, three, four of them. The Navahos were strung out in single file, a warrior carrying a lance in the lead, his head held low as he scanned the ground. Fargo marveled at the man's ability to track so well in the dark. Keep on coming! he urged mentally, pleased his trap was working.

Then, from the direction of the saguaros where Thomas and the three women were hidden, there came a distinct cough.

14

The Navahos immediately reined up and became mounted statues, their faces turned toward the cactuses screening the four Shakers.

Fargo wanted to throttle whoever had been so careless. He expected the warriors to alter their course and ride directly toward the spot where the cough originated, which would make his plan useless. They would pass him, but they wouldn't pass Caleb and Chilton. Sure enough, the leader started forward, turning his horse to the east, and the rest did the same.

He couldn't let them reach the women. Even though it meant tangling with all four by himself, he had to stop them. The foremost warrior now held the lance at shoulder height, ready to hurl it in the blink of an eye. The second warrior held a bow, while the third and the fourth both carried war clubs. Fargo's strategy was dictated by their weapons. Since the man with the lance and the warrior with the bow posed the deadliest threats, he would slay them first.

The lead rider passed within eight feet of Fargo's hiding place. He let the man go for the moment so the second warrior could draw abreast of his position. Then he sprang into action, bursting from cover even as he snapped the rifle to his shoulder and sighted on the leader's back. Ordinarily he detested the idea of back-shooting anyone, but given the circumstances he couldn't afford the luxury of attacking the Navahos head-on.

The man in the lead started to look back as the rifle cracked, the shot striking him between the shoulder blades and knocking him forward to fall over his mount's shoulder.

Fargo didn't dare wait to see if the man was dead. He kept going, reaching the second Navaho at the selfsame instant the warrior elevated the bow to take aim. Thrusting both arms out and up, Fargo rammed the barrel into the man's gut with enough force to topple the rider to the ground. The horse, spooked, ran on, and Fargo closed in on the rising Navaho, swinging the rifle in a tight arc. The heavy barrel struck the warrior across the forehead and dropped him in his tracks.

Whooping savagely, the remaining pair galloped to the aid of their fellows.

In a flash Fargo had the throwing knife in his right hand and swept his arm overhead. The third Navaho screeched, waving his war club in the air, and léaned down to deliver a cranium-crushing blow. But Fargo was quicker. He hurled the toothpick as he had countless times before, in a smooth motion that sent the blade into the Navaho's chest, the knife sinking in to the hilt.

Stiffening, the third warrior clutched at the weapon and rode on past.

That left the fourth Navaho, who had prudently learned from the fate of his friends not to be hasty, and who slowed to ensure that the swing of his war club was right on target.

Fargo ducked and darted to the right, hearing the swish of the club as it narrowly missed his head. Then he whirled and leaped, thinking the Navaho would halt and turn, intending to employ the rifle as a club. The Navaho, however, thwarted him by continuing eastward. Not only that, the warrior commenced shouting and flailing his arms.

The reason became crystal clear. Goaded by the shouts, the three other horses were fleeing into the night. The warrior who had taken the knife in the chest swayed precariously, then tumbled to the earth.

Stopping in midstride, racked by frustration, Fargo watched the surviving Navaho vanish into the gloom with the trio of riderless horses. A scream cut the night, and he raced ahead to find the women and Thomas standing in the open and gazing after the departing warrior. "Anyone hurt?" he asked.

"No," Naomi said. "I screamed because I thought that heathen was going to ride me down."

The Navaho was two dozen yards away. He looked over his shoulder before the darkness swallowed him and shook his war club at them.

"How many did you get?" Thomas asked Fargo.

"Three," Fargo answered, and suddenly remembered the

Navaho he'd bashed with the rifle. The man was probably still alive. Spinning, he ran back to where the warrior lay.

All of the Shakers converged on him on the run.

"We didn't have a chance to help," Caleb protested. "Why did you hog the job for yourself?"

"It couldn't be helped. Someone coughed and gave us away," Fargo answered, and gave each of the four prime suspects a withering glare.

"I did," Thomas said sheepishly.

"You could have gotten us all killed."

"I know. I'm sorry," Thomas said. "It just sort of came out. My throat was dry, and I did the first thing that came into my head."

"The next time you might get an arrow in the head," Fargo said testily.

"There's no need to be angry with Thomas," Naomi said. "Everything worked out fine, didn't it? There's only one Navaho left and he'll head back to his village. By the time he can return with others, we should be long gone."

"You hope," Fargo said. Logically, she was right. But a vague feeling of unease gnawed at the back of his mind, as if there was something he was overlooking, something that would bode ill in the near future.

The unconscious Navaho groaned.

Fargo began reloading the rifle. He looked at Caleb as he worked. "My knife is sticking in the last brave who fell. Would you get it for me?"

"My pleasure," the skinny Shaker said, moving off.

Naomi was studying the big man. "You like this, don't you, Mr. Fargo?"

"Beg pardon, ma'am?"

"You must like killing. From what I can tell, you're very good at it. And it doesn't seem to bother you in the least. I would imagine you view taking a human life the same way most people regard squashing a bug," Naomi elaborated.

"How can you say such a terrible thing?" Gretchen came to Fargo's defense. "He's doing his best to get us out of this awful desert and all you do is criticize him."

"She's right," Chilton threw in. "You have no call to be carping on him the way you are."

Naomi sniffed. "I would expect the two of you to defend him, but I see him in a different light. Your precious Mr. Fargo is an example of all that's wrong with our world. He's a violent man who spreads violence wherever he goes. And didn't we join the Shakers to escape such a horrid way of life? To remove ourselves from people like him?"

"A person can't run away from the world," Fargo commented. "You accuse me of being violent, but this is a violent land. West of the Mississippi there are two classes of men, the quick and the dead. And I don't aim to join the ranks of the dead for quite some spell."

"So you justify your violence in the name of self-preservation?" Naomi said. "How quaint."

Fargo wished she were a man so he could lay a good one on her jaw. "What the hell is quaint about wanting to live? Out here a person can go around minding his own business and still find himself on the business end of a gun. Look at what happened to your leader."

"The only way to respond to violence is with kindness," Naomi stated. "The meek shall inherit the earth."

"Maybe," Fargo said, "but they sure as blazes ain't about to inherit the West."

The argument was interrupted by the return of Caleb, who handed over the Arkansas toothpick. Fargo finished reloading just as the Navaho groaned again and opened his eyes.

"Oh, my," Ruth breathed.

"Howdy," Fargo said, touching the muzzle to the tip of the warrior's angular nose. "Do you speak the white man's tongue?"

The Indian blinked, his gaze glued to the rifle. "Yes," he replied softly. "A little."

"Good. It'll make this easier," Fargo said, and leaned lower to accent his next statement. "Make one move I don't like and I'll send you to meet your ancestors. Savvy?"

"Yes," the Navaho said.

"What's your handle?"

"I not understand."

"Your name. What is your name?"

"I am called Spotted Horse."

Fargo backed up, keeping the rifle trained on the warrior's torso, and motioned for him to rise. "On your feet and turn around."

The Navaho obeyed, displaying no nervousness whatsoever. He wore beaded buckskins and moccasins. His dark hair hung past his shoulders.

"Put your hands behind your back," Fargo directed.

Again the warrior complied.

"What are you planning to do?" Naomi asked suspiciously.

"Tie his hands so he can't give us any trouble," Fargo responded, and looked down at the hem of her dress. "Since we didn't bring any rope, we'll have to cut the bottom two inches off of your dress."

Naomi took a step backward. "You will not," she flatly refused. "No article of mine will be used for immoral ends."

"We need something to tie him with," Fargo said.

"Give me a knife," Gretchen said. "I'll cut the material off of my dress." She glanced at Naomi. "Now that my eyes have been opened, I find it incredible that I once respected you for your wisdom. No wonder you joined the Shakers. You wouldn't last a month in the real world."

Insulted, Naomi turned on her heel and walked off a few yards. Ruth accompanied her.

Fargo waited while Caleb gave his knife to Gretchen and she swiftly removed her hem and another inch besides. Then he nodded at Caleb. "Remove his quiver. Then tie his wrists tight. We don't want to wake up tomorrow afternoon with our throats slit."

"I'll truss this Injun like a hog being taken to slaughter," Caleb said gleefully, and took delight in binding the Navaho's arm from the wrists to the elbows as tightly as he could, securing the many loops with three large knots. "There," he said, moving to one side. "He won't break free of that for a month of Sundays."

"Pick up his bow and arrows," Fargo instructed. "They might come in handy later." He faced Chilton. "Gather the weapons from the dead Navahos. We'll take them with us also."

"Yes, sir," Chilton said, hastening to perform the task.

Thomas cleared his throat. "I won't carry a weapon, Mr. Fargo, no matter what you want."

"You'll be carrying the water bag," Fargo reminded him.

The young Shaker held out his empty hands and gawked at them in disbelief. "Oh, my goodness. I left it back where we were hiding."

"Get it," Fargo growled. He was eager to resume their trek. By morning they must find somewhere suitable to hole up for the day, preferably somewhere out of the sun so the heat wouldn't dry their bodies and fry their brains. He grabbed the Navaho's bound wrists and pointed the warrior northward. "Start walking," he said, and fell in behind him. "I'm leaving," he called out. "Anyone who wants to come, can."

"Wait for me!" Thomas yelled from off in the saguaros.

But Fargo didn't wait. It would teach the Shaker a lesson, he figured, by making him hurry to catch them. The others formed a single file once more, Chilton carrying both a lance and a war club. Caleb had slung the quiver over his back and held the bow in his left hand.

They hadn't gone fifteen yards when Thomas, panting and clutching the water bag with both arms, sprinted out of the cactuses and took the last place in line.

Gretchen laughed. "I've never seen him move so fast," she told Fargo.

"If we run into more Navahos, he'll move a darn sight faster," Fargo predicted.

"Do you really think we will?"

"There's no telling," Fargo said, still bothered by the vague premonition of impending trouble.

They hiked in silence for the next hour and a half. Fargo pushed the pace, constantly surveying the terrain for a place to stop for the day. It would be dawn soon, and once the sun rose the desert would be transformed into an inferno. But all he saw was flat land in all directions.

His features hardened when a golden tinge rimmed the eastern horizon. They had half an hour at the most, and then the temperature would rise dramatically. He noticed a low rise about eighty yards to the northeast and made toward it. If better cover was unavailable, they could dig a narrow trench in which to shield themselves from the blistering rays of the sun. Unfortunately, without proper tools and given the hard soil they must deal with, it would take a few hours to complete. By then they would be sweltering.

He went to the rise because he hoped to find looser earth on it's six-foot-high slopes. Instead, when he stepped to the top, he discovered the rise was actually the rim of a ravine that extended for several hundred feet in both directions. The sides rose over thirty feet from the ravine floor and were too steep to climb.

Fargo went to the right, seeking a way to the bottom, and finally found it at the end of the ravine, where a gradual incline led down into its depths. He gestured for the Shakers to precede him. They wearily trudged into the ravine, Naomi, Ruth, and Thomas shuffling their feet as if on their last legs. Fargo followed, gazing eastward to see the fiery crown of the sun appear.

The Shakers had only advanced fifteen yards. Gretchen had stopped, so they all halted.

Prodding the Navaho with the rifle, Fargo hurried along the line. "What's the holdup?" he demanded when he was close to the lovely blonde.

Gretchen didn't answer. She didn't have to. From in front of her arose the ominous rattling of a sidewinder.

15

Taking a step to the left, Fargo spied the deadly reptile. That's when he saw it wasn't a true sidewinder, which always possessed triangular, hornlike projections over each eye, but instead was a large specimen of the variety of vipers known to naturalists as Western Diamondback Rattlesnakes and to ordinary folks simply as diamondheads. Cousins to the sidewinders, diamondbacks were much more aggressive. Some folks claimed they were the nastiest of all rattlers.

This one exceeded six and a half feet in length. Its thick back bore patterns resembling black diamonds with light borders. Broad white and black rings encircled its tail just below its twelve vibrating rattles.

In typical diamondback fashion when about to strike, the body was tightly coiled and its head was held high above those coils as its forked tongue repeatedly flicked out from its wicked maw.

All this Fargo took in the moment he laid eyes on the snake. Since diamondbacks were mainly nocturnal, he figured the reptile had been on its way to its den when Gretchen stumbled upon it. With the rattler poised to sink its fangs into her, he couldn't try to distract it or drive it off. He must act immediately.

He sighted on the reptile's head, cocked the plains rifle, and stroked the trigger. In the confines of the ravine the discharge was deafening. The slug struck the diamondback between its eyes and bored straight through its head, spattering blood and brains all over its coils. Whipped backward by the impact, the diamondback flopped onto the ground and convulsed, its tail still rattling.

Fargo took a step closer, his right hand on the throwing knife in case the reptile was still alive. Suddenly Gretchen was in his arms, clinging to him in grateful joy, her eyes closed as her lips spoke the same two words over and over.

"Thank you. Thank you. Thank you."

"You've got to watch where you walk in the desert," Fargo admonished her. In response, she pecked him on the cheek and squeezed him with all her might.

"I didn't see it until the last second," Gretchen replied after a bit, and let go.

Fargo stepped up to the snake and went to kick the creature aside. Then an idea hit him and he changed his mind. He leaned down and picked it up.

"What are you doing?" Chilton asked.

"We'll need food later," Fargo said.

"Oh, goodness," Gretchen murmured. "I don't know if I could bring myself to eat a snake. Particularly a rattlesnake."

"They're right tasty," Fargo informed her. "Even raw."

"Raw?" she repeated, aghast.

Chilton grimaced. "I seriously doubt whether any of us would stoop to eating such fare, friend."

"When a person is hungry enough they'll eat anything," Fargo said, and draped the limp snake over his left shoulder. "Since I happen to like rattler, I aim to help myself, and if any of you change your minds you'll be welcome to a share of the meat."

"Never!" young Thomas declared.

Shrugging, Fargo motioned for the Navaho to take the lead and stayed on his heels. They advanced another thirty yards until they reached a point where the ravine narrowed to a mere six feet in width. The sheer walls overhead blocked out the sunlight. Fargo nodded in satisfaction. This was just what he'd wanted. They could sit out the day in relative comfort and be fresh for another night of hard travel by sundown. "Pick a spot and make yourselves comfortable," he announced, turning. "This is where we'll stay until evening."

Wearing expressions of relief, the Shakers settled down, most sitting with their backs to a wall for greater comfort. Thomas propped the water bag at his side.

The Navaho remained standing.

"You can take a seat if you want," Fargo told him, and lowered himself to the ground with a profound sigh.

"I stand," Spotted Horse stated defiantly.

"Your choice," Fargo said, "but if you don't get any rest and you can't keep up tonight, I'll be obliged to put a bullet in you so you can't run off and alert any other Navahos in the area."

Then the Navaho did a strange thing. He smiled slyly.

Puzzled, Fargo studied the man. Why did he do that? Was it because there *were* more Navahos around? Counting Spotted Horse, the one who got away last night, and the six warriors slain so far, he'd accounted for the eight he'd seen shortly after Delgado dumped him in the desert and rode off. He recollected the smoke signal they had seen and—

The smoke signal!

A tingle rippled down Fargo's spine. He wanted to slap himself for being the biggest goldarned fool to ever wear britches. The eight warriors he'd seen had been responsible for sending the smoke signal, and they sure as hell weren't signaling themselves. So there had to be more Navahos in the vicinity. Maybe the eight were just part of a larger war party. If so, where were the others?

Another idea occurred to him. What if the Navahos had come to the Jornada del Muerto for a reason other than attacking the Shakers' wagon train? He knew that Indians used a wide variety of herbal remedies and that some of the plants from which the cures were extracted only grew in the desert. Then again, the Navahos were partial to turquoise and the other stones that were reputed to be found in the Jornada del Muerto.

Fargo looked at the captive. "What brought your band to this region?" he asked, then placed the dead snake on the ground.

Spotted Horse spoke a Navaho word, then corrected himself. "Blue stones, those that bring us good luck."

Turquoise, Fargo reflected, and gestured at the Shakers. "So you had no idea these folks were in this area when you came?"

"No. We much surprised to find them. Whites not come here often."

So the Shakers had had the misfortune of being in the wrong place at the wrong time. Fargo stared at them, thinking of all the lives that had been lost because they wanted to find somewhere free from violence and hatred. If they had stayed back in Ohio, where they were safe and sound, none of this would have happened.

Spotted Horse took a few steps and sat. "Who are you, white eyes?"

Fargo told him.

"You not like others," the Navaho said, nodding at the Shakers. "They are weak. You strong like Indian."

"I've lived with Indians," Fargo said. "I know your ways very well and I admire the Indian way of life."

"Not many whites think like you," Spotted Horse said. "Most hate my people. Most think we are animals." He paused and held his head high. "We are the People."

Fargo had heard the term before. The Navahos called themselves the People of the Way, referring to the proper path they must follow between the cradle and the grave. They believed their lives were controlled by spirit beings known as the Holy People, and if they strayed from the path the Holy People dictated they would face dire calamities.

"I have heard that the People are making more and more trouble for the whites," Fargo said. "If this keeps up, the whites will send their army to crush the Navahos."

Spotted Horse laughed. "This not happen. The People are strong, stronger than all whites put together. We will drive your kind from our land."

"Never happen," Fargo assured him. "If the Navaho don't stop raiding and killing, they will end up like the Seminoles, the Choctaws, and the Cherokees, tribes who lived far to the east near the great ocean."

"Where are they now?"

"The white government forced them to leave their lands and march many miles to the region the whites now call Indian Territory. Hundreds died on the march. They lost everything because they wouldn't live in peace," Fargo related. "The Navahos will one day lose everything too."

"Pardon me," Gretchen interrupted. "Is it all right for me to drink some water?"

"Yes," Naomi added. "We're terribly thirsty. It's starting to become quite hot."

Fargo glanced up at the bright azure sky. "It's a lot hotter up there," he remarked, and stood. His own throat was dry. It was too bad he must restrict each of them to a single swallow if the water was to last until they were out of the desert. "I reckon we could all use some," he said, and walked toward Thomas. The young Shaker was resting with his forearms draped over his knees and his forehead on his arms. "Are you awake?" he inquired.

Thomas didn't move.

"Plumb tuckered out," Fargo remarked, and looked at the water bag. A chill pierced his chest. There was a moist stain all around the bottom of the bag. "No!" he cried, and reached it in two bounds, his cry startling Thomas, who sat up with a start and looked around in confusion. Fargo released the rifle so he could grab the bag with both hands and lift it, and he gaped down in shock when water splashed onto his leggings and moccasins, soaking them.

"What's happening?" Thomas blurted out.

Fargo turned the bag around, hearing gasps from several of the others at the sight of a large, ragged hole near the bottom. He glanced at the spot where Thomas had placed the bag and saw the small, irregular stone spike that had made the hole.

"You're spilling the water," Thomas said, still unaware of the hole.

Fargo dropped to his knees and turned the bag upside down so the remaining water would sink into the intact portion. From the size of the puddle at the base of the wall, a puddle that was rapidly being soaked up by the parched soil, he guessed that most of their water was now gone. He groped the bag with his right hand, confirming his hunch. Less than two inches of the precious fluid remained.

"What happened?" Thomas asked again.

The other Shakers were gathering around, their faces etched in shock.

"Dear Lord!" Chilton exclaimed.

"Not the water!" Ruth said.

Fargo bowed his head, struggling to control his surging rage. He suddenly straightened and gave the bag to Caleb, then whirled and bent over to grab Thomas by the front of his shirt.

"You damned greenhorn!" he snapped, hauling the man upright. "Do you have any idea of what you've done?"

Blinking in bewilderment, Thomas said, "I don't understand. What did I do that has you so mad?"

"Look!" Fargo said, and jabbed a finger at the stone spike. "You didn't check to see if it was safe to set the bag down. You poked a hole in it. Now we barely have any water left."

"Oh," Thomas said softly, horrified at what he had done.

Chilton placed a hand on Fargo's arm. "Please, friend, let him go. He didn't think, that's all."

"Out here a man who doesn't think doesn't live long," Fargo said, his rage subsiding as abruptly as it had flared. He relaxed his fingers and stepped back. Blaming the young Shaker for the loss would accomplish nothing. He'd known the Shakers were bound to be a bother; he just hadn't counted on something so major as losing most of their water.

"I didn't mean to do it," Thomas said sorrowfully. "Brother Amos is right. I set the bag down without thinking."

Caleb hefted the bag, listening to the water slosh around inside. "Can we make it to Adobe Wells with this little left?"

"We have to make it, water or no water," Fargo responded, and drew his knife.

"What are you aiming to do?" Thomas asked, recoiling in fear. "I'm sorry. I'm truly sorry."

"I'm not about to stick you," Fargo said, and extended the knife toward Gretchen. "Will you cut another strip from your dress? We need to tie the bag shut below the hole so the rest of the water doesn't evaporate before we drink it."

"Gladly," she said, taking the toothpick and bending down.

Fargo handled the tying himself when she was done. He squeezed the bag under the hole until the bunched up leather was as thick around as his wrist, then looped the fabric around the makeshift neck several times before binding the material tight.

"How about if I'm in charge of the bag from now on?" Caleb volunteered.

"No, give it to me," Thomas said. "I deserve a second chance."

Fargo shook his head and gave the bag to Caleb. "I'm not making the same mistake twice."

"What about that drink you promised us?" Naomi asked.

"Sorry, folks. We'll hold off until the sun is directly above us," Fargo said.

"Can't we even have a sip?" Naomi persisted in her usual testy manner.

"No."

Naomi rubbed her throat and licked her lips. "I don't see how you expect us to survive without at least a sip. A person can't live without water."

"Now you're beginning to catch on," Fargo said. "It would be best if all of you lie down and try to sleep. We'll be up all night again tonight."

Gretchen turned, running her right hand through her hair. "I could sleep for a week," she said, then stopped short. "Say, Skye?"

"What?"

"Where's the Navaho?"

Fargo pivoted, flabbergasted to see that the prisoner had flown the coop. He glimpsed the warrior several dozen yards down the ravine, fleeing like a bounding buck toward the far end and freedom.

16

"Why, that heathen is getting away," Naomi said in a tone that implied she was shocked by the Navaho's audacity.

Fargo went to retrieve the rifle, then remembered he'd failed to reload it after shooting the diamondback. He snatched the Arkansas toothpick from Gretchen's hand, then took off in pursuit, marveling at the speed and agility the warrior demonstrated even with bound arms.

Spotted Horse looked back, saw Fargo coming on fast, and grinned.

Fargo chided himself for being so careless. He shouldn't have let the incident with the water bag distract him from the prisoner. Being up all night had dulled his mind, he concluded, and he resolved to get some sleep at the first opportunity. But first he had to catch Spotted Horse, and the Navaho wasn't going to make it easy on him. He could recollect few men so fleet of foot.

Scattered along the bottom of the ravine at random intervals were boulders of varying sizes, some no bigger than a boot, others as large as a saddle. Fargo threaded his way among them, leaping over the smaller ones, and did everything he could to narrow the gap. Try as he might, his legs pumping furiously, he gained little ground on the Navaho.

To make matters worse, he commenced sweating profusely. It was cooler in the ravine, but not *that* much cooler, and the exertion was taking a toll on his already weary body. Losing so much moisture was a severe drain on the physical constitution. Under normal circumstances it wasn't serious, but in the desert, and lacking water to replace the loss, it might have grave consequences later on.

Fargo wondered what the Navaho had in mind. They were, so far as he knew, far from any water hole. If Spotted Horse should escape, where would the man go? Granted, Indians were hardier than whites and extremely knowledgeable about wilderness lore, but even Indians had their limits, and without water they were as much handicapped in desert travel as their white counterparts. Indians could no more wander aimlessly over the desert and expect to survive than anyone else could. He suspected the Navaho had a specific destination in mind, somewhere that could be reached on foot, which meant somewhere close. Perhaps somewhere water could be found.

The warrior was still running strong, exhibiting outstanding endurance. He ran with a slightly bent posture, turning his arms to the right or the left whenever he swung around a boulder, depending on which way he was turning.

Fargo saw a bend up ahead. Spotted Horse disappeared past it, and Fargo was forced to slow as he neared it as a precaution in case the Navaho should be waiting on the other side to jump him. He held the knife, point out, at his waist, and kept his back near the off wall when he went around the bend. Then he halted in amazement and did a double take.

Spotted Horse was gone.

Fargo scanned the length of the ravine and saw no sign of the Navaho. There were no other bends, and none of the boulders dotting the bottom were large enough for a man to hide behind. Where the blazes could the Indian have gone?

He warily jogged forward, suspecting a trick, scouring both sides for a recessed perch the warrior might use to ambush him. But the sides were essentially smooth. Mystified, Fargo covered ten more yards before the mystery was solved. To his right appeared a break in the ravine wall, a narrow defile with an inclined bottom, an earthen ramp, that went all the way up to the rim of the ravine.

Freshly imprinted in the dusty soil were moccasin tracks.

Fargo rushed up the defile and paused near the top to peek out. He half expected the warrior to be waiting for him, ready to kick his head off, but Spotted Horse was dozens of yards away, fleeing across the open, scorching desert.

"Damn," Fargo muttered, and burst out of the defile, giving chase. He felt the full heat of the sun the instant he emerged. In the span of four strides he began sweating twice as much as before. It was enough to tempt him to turn around and go back, but he couldn't allow the Navaho to get away. So he raced onward, his clothes becoming soaked and plastered to his skin.

Spotted Horse had been heading due north. Now he changed direction, running to the northwest, and began yelling in his native tongue.

There could be only one explanation. Fargo gazed past the warrior but saw barren desert and nothing else. There was no one out there to hear the Navaho's yells.

Or was there?

Fargo almost halted in consternation when he spied a number of figures far, far off on the horizon. Riders, they were, and although he couldn't determine their identities he could make a good guess. They were more Navahos, and if they heard Spotted Horse the Shakers would be in grave jeopardy. He tried to run faster, but he was already pushing his body to its limit.

Spotted Horse started jumping into the air every few strides, a human antelope hoping to attract the attention of the riders.

Reversing his grip on the knife, Fargo toyed with the idea of hurling it. The range was too great at the moment. All he had to do was gain ten yards and he could try his desperate gambit.

The figures on the horizon were distorted by the shimmering waves of heat cast off by the desert soil. It was impossible to count them, even to know if they were indeed Indians. One fact was certain, however. They were slowly drawing nearer.

Fargo despaired of ever overtaking the Navaho. His own legs were on the verge of collapse and his lungs ached horribly. He wasn't a quitter by nature, but he knew a losing cause when he saw one. He had no hope of catching the warrior.

Suddenly Spotted Horse tripped and crashed to the earth, smashing onto his stomach. He lay there, dazed and wheezing, the breath knocked out of him.

So much for no hope. Fargo goaded his flagging muscles to greater speed and was fifteen feet from the Navaho when Spotted Horse finally struggled to his knees and twisted, hatred replacing his cocky expression. The warrior lowered his head and surged up like a charging bull.

Fargo evaded the first rush by adroitly sidestepping to the right. He flicked his right leg out, his foot hooking the Navaho's left ankle, and Spotted Horse stumbled and almost fell. Catlike, the warrior recovered his balance and whirled.

"Give it up," Fargo advised, wagging the knife.

Spotted Horse glanced at the distant riders, then snarled, "Never!" He charged again.

Anxious to end the fight, Fargo shifted to the left and punched the Navaho in the gut, doubling Spotted Horse over. Still game, Spotted Horse tried to kick Fargo in the knee but missed by a fraction of an inch. Fargo slammed the knife hilt onto the tip of the warrior's jaw, rocking the man on his heels, and kneed him where it would do the most damage.

Sputtering, Spotted Horse collapsed onto his back. He crossed his legs and groaned.

Fargo bent down and pressed the point of the toothpick to the warrior's throat. "That's just a taste of what you'll get if you give me another lick of trouble."

Spotted Horse took deep breaths and glared.

"On your feet," Fargo directed, moving back to give himself room to wield the knife should the Navaho resist further. If he had any brains he would kill the man and be done with it, but he wasn't a cold-blooded murderer and slaying someone who had his arms tied amounted to the same thing.

Reluctantly, slowly, Spotted Horse obeyed.

"Now head for the ravine and keep low," Fargo told him. To accent the order, he jabbed the Navaho in the neck, a prick that broke the skin and drew a little blood.

Spotted Horse cast a longing gaze at the far-off riders, then turned and retraced his steps.

Stepping sideways so he could keep an eye on the approaching figures, Fargo had to prod the Navaho along. When they came to the gap, the riders were still too far off to note details. "Down you go," Fargo said, and gave Spotted Horse a shove to hurry him.

The warrior almost pitched onto his face. He caught himself and went halfway to the bottom, then halted and looked up. "You soon be dead, white man."

"Are those riders friends of yours?" Fargo asked, stopping with just his head above the edge so he could observe the band's progress.

"From my village, yes," Spotted Horse answered.

"I hate to disappoint you, but I don't think they saw us," Fargo said.

"No. But they see tracks."

Fargo could see the trail of footprints extending from the ravine to the spot where they'd tussled, and if those Navahos came within twenty feet of the prints then they would see them also. He didn't doubt for a minute that they were who Spotted Horse claimed they were. If they did find the tracks, he would have to lead them away from the Shakers.

The vague shapes solidified into seven warriors. They were clustered in a group, talking and smiling, clearly unaware that anyone else was within a hundred miles of them. And they were traveling from the northwest to the southeast.

Would they pass close to the footprints? Fargo lowered his head until his eyes were at the rim. His intuition flared, and he glanced at Spotted Horse at the very moment the warrior opened his mouth to shout. The yell would draw the band, and there was no way Fargo could stop the man in time. In pure reflex, he took a step toward the warrior and swept the knife overhead to throw it.

Spotted Horse froze, staring at the glittering blade, his mouth wide. He looked into the big man's eyes.

Fargo knew what the brave was thinking. "One peep out of you and you're dead," he vowed. "Your friends might get us, but you won't be around to see it." He waited, his nerves tingling, keenly aware that his life and the lives of the Shakers hung in the balance. Everything depended on whether the Navaho believed him or not.

Shoulders slumping, Spotted Horse closed his mouth and scowled. "I not ready to die," he said.

"Smart hombre," Fargo responded, and checked on the riders again. They were over a hundred yards away, bearing to the southeast, and would not even come close to the tracks. He moved down the incline and gestured for Spotted Horse to precede him. They walked back in silence.

The Shakers were all on their feet, anxiously waiting his return. Caleb cradled the water bag as if it were a lover. Chilton held the empty rifle. Naomi, once she saw that the Navaho had been recaptured, yawned and sat down. Ruth and Thomas simply stood there.

Gretchen clasped her slender hands to her delicate throat and beamed. "I was so worried," she said. "I thought something had happened to you."

"This varmint tried his best," Fargo said, and slapped the warrior on the shoulder. "Sit down and don't budge if you know what's good for you."

Spotted Horse complied.

"You were gone a long time," Chilton noted, bringing the rifle over.

"There are more Navahos out there," Fargo announced, sliding the knife into its sheath and taking the gun. He immediately set about reloading.

"How many?" Chilton asked.

"Where are they?" Caleb threw in.

"They were north of us a ways," Fargo informed him. "There are seven, all told. I figure they've already passed the ravine and should be well on their way to wherever they're headed."

"Want one of us to check?" Caleb inquired.

Young Thomas moved forward. "I'll do it," he offered eagerly.

"I'll go myself," Fargo said.

"Please. I'd like to make up for losing most of the water. Let me do something," Thomas pleaded.

Although it was against Fargo's better judgment, he nodded. Holding a grudge indefinitely was a waste of energy. "Go to the end of the ravine, where we came in," he instructed. "And whatever you do, don't let them see you."

"I won't, friend."

Fargo watched the young man hasten off, then sighed and squatted. After his exertions, he sorely craved water. He figured the Shakers would need it even more later, so he contented himself with licking his dry lips and imagining what it would be like to take a plunge into a cool mountain lake.

"I don't see how you expect us to sleep in this heat, Mr. Fargo," Naomi complained, fanning her neck with her hand.

"And you folks thought you'd find paradise here," Fargo said, and laughed. "You'd be better off staking a claim in a Florida swamp."

"I went there once."

"*I* was born there," Naomi said.

The sudden drumming of footsteps brought Fargo to his feet with the rifle leveled. Thomas ran up to them and stopped, panting as he motioned toward the end of the ravine.

"We have a problem!" he exclaimed.

"What sort of problem?" Fargo demanded.

"I went up to have a look, and those Indians weren't as far away as you said they'd be. In fact, they were stopped about sixty yards out and one of them was examining a hoof on his horse," Thomas reported.

"And!" Fargo prompted, glancing at the rim, dreading the answer he was certain to receive.

"They saw me."

17

Naomi placed both hands on her hips and snapped at the youngest Shaker. "Honestly, Brother Thomas, how could you be so careless?"

Fargo grabbed Gretchen by the arm and shoved her toward the opposite end of the ravine. "We've got to move! Run as fast as your legs will carry you!" Gretchen obeyed instantly. Caleb and Chilton followed her.

The rest hesitated.

"I'm too tired to run a step," Naomi said, gazing upward. "Besides, there's no sign of the Indians. Maybe Brother Thomas was wrong. Maybe they didn't spot him."

"This is no time to be arguing," Fargo said angrily, moving toward her. "Head out now or your hide won't be worth a plugged nickel."

"Rubbish," Naomi said.

An arrow whizzed out of the blue and thudded into Naomi's chest, driving her back against the wall, where she stood for a moment with her arms outflung and her features reflecting profound astonishment. A second shaft streaked down, tearing into the base of her throat, and blood welled up out of her mouth.

Fargo didn't wait to see her fall. He had been standing in the shadows and now he stepped out, sweeping the rifle upward, and discovered two Navahos standing on the rim. Both had bows. One of them loosed another shaft and Fargo heard Ruth scream. Then he fired, his shot striking the same warrior in the stomach and doubling the man over. The second Navaho ducked from view. With the gun empty and useless, Fargo back-pedaled, catching sight of Thomas lying in the dirt, an arrow jutting out of the young Shaker's left eye.

Ruth stood to one side, in shock, her hands over her mouth, tears pouring down her cheeks as she gawked at Thomas.

"Come on," Fargo growled, seizing her wrist and yanking her along. "We're sitting ducks down here. We've got to move." He broke into a run but only managed to go a few yards when Ruth dug in her heels and wrenched her wrist from his grip. "What the—" Fargo began, shifting.

An arrow angled upward from between Ruth's shoulder blades, its sharp point buried somewhere in her chest. She gulped air, her limbs going slack as her eyelids fluttered.

Fargo tried to grab her, but gravity was quicker. Down she went, onto her back, breaking the arrow in half. He surveyed the rim, thinking he would be the next target. The second Navaho was temporarily gone and there was no sign of the rest. He looked at Ruth, wondering if there was something he could do. Her blank, glassy stare told him otherwise.

Fargo ran. He felt like an animal in a trap, and he knew he would be lucky to get out of there alive. He was outnumbered, hemmed in by the ravine walls, and handicapped because the Navahos held the high ground. He went twenty yards and came to a point where a partial overhang would screen him from the Indians. Moving under it, he swiftly began reloading.

He hoped Gretchen and the others were all right. As much as he wanted to keep going, he wouldn't be able to protect them with an empty gun. He suddenly realized that Spotted Horse had again disappeared in the confusion, and he figured the devious warrior had already rejoined the rest of the band.

Fargo wondered if Spotted Horse had told the truth about the reason the Navahos were in the Jornada del Muerto. When he took into account the eleven that initially attacked the Shaker wagon train and the seven up above, it made a grand total of eighteen men, far more than were needed to gather turquoise. He suspected the band had a twofold purpose: gathering the blue stones and conducting a few raids on the side. There were a number of ranches to the northeast and northwest of the Jornada del Muerto, prime targets for the marauding Navahos.

The rifle reloaded, Fargo dashed from concealment and sprinted along the floor of the ravine. He didn't see Gretchen, Caleb, or Chilton, and assumed they had a commanding lead. Then he reached the narrow gap that rose to the desert proper and heard a scream of terror.

Up he went, the rifle stock tucked to his shoulder, and darted out into the blistering sunshine. He glimpsed Caleb to his right, pierced by three arrows. To his left lay Chilton, his throat pumping crimson, the victim of a lance. And riding hard to the north were seven Navahos, one of whom was Spotted Horse. He also saw Gretchen astride one of the war horses, held in the firm grip of a tall warrior.

Fuming, Fargo took careful aim, sighting on the back of the brave riding beside Gretchen's captor. It was too risky to shoot the tall warrior, because the slug might pass through him and bury itself into her. The hammer felt cool to his touch as he thumbed it back until it clicked. Taking a breath, he steadied the heavy barrel, then fired.

Two hundred yards out the Navaho threw up his arms and toppled from his mount.

The others looked back. None had rifles, and they couldn't hope to get close enough to empty their bows before losing one or two men to the powerful plains rifle. The tall warrior spoke and they all lashed their horses, galloping off in a cloud of dust, trying to get out of range.

Fargo frantically reloaded, wishing he had his Sharps. The old single-shots were cumbersome, took too long to load, and didn't pack as hard a wallop. It took him forty seconds to cram a ball and powder into Caleb's weapon, and by then the Navahos were scores of yards farther away and hidden by the dust raised in their wake.

He didn't bother to fire. There was no sense in wasting ammunition when he would need it later. He went to Caleb and verified the skinny Shaker was dead. The arrows had pierced the water bag before ripping into Caleb's wiry body, and the water was now seeping into the parched soil. He checked the bag anyway but saw no water inside.

Incensed at the turn of events, Fargo walked over to Chilton. The Shaker wore a peaceful expression. Death, evidently, had been met with courage and the belief that a better life awaited beyond. Fargo frowned and gazed after the departing Navahos. Something moved in the dust cloud, and seconds later a riderless horse appeared.

Hope flooded through Fargo. It was the horse that had

belonged to the last Navaho he'd shot. In their rush to get away, the other Navahos had plumb forgotten about it. Or maybe none of them had cared to ride back for it and expose himself to Fargo's rifle. Whatever, that animal was his salvation if he could get his hands on it.

He jogged northward, watching the horse ride up to the fallen warrior and nudge the man with its muzzle. Loyalty in man or beast was a trait Fargo admired. This particular cayuse must be a fine animal to show such devotion. It looked up as he drew nearer, its ears pricked toward him, and he feared it would run off.

"I won't harm you," Fargo said softly, slowing. He held the rifle behind his back so the odor of the gunpowder wouldn't spook the animal. "Easy, boy," he added. "Take it easy."

The horse, a brown stallion, backed up several steps and snorted.

Fargo slowed to a walk and plastered a smile on his lips. "I'm your friend," he said. "All I want is a ride."

Again the animal retreated nervously.

Could it be the strange language the horse didn't like? Fargo mused, and changed to the Sioux tongue, the Indian language he knew best of all. It was only slightly similar to Navaho, but it wouldn't sound as alien as English.

The cayuse tilted its head and stamped a hoof.

"Let me touch you," Fargo said softly. He slowly extended his right hand. Any abrupt moves now would defeat his purpose, would scare the animal into racing off. "You are a fine horse and must have made your owner very happy."

Not so much as a muscle twitched. The stallion didn't even blink.

"I would like to ride you," Fargo said. His fingers were inches from the war bridle, and he was tempted to lunge for it. He controlled himself and gently grasped the rope, then stepped up close, wedged the rifle between his legs, and began stroking the animal's neck and rubbing it behind the ears. "See, I'm your friend."

Fargo petted the stallion for several minutes until he believed the horse had accepted him. Gripping the reins, he swung onto its back and braced for a bucking. The animal simply stood still, perfectly under control. His ploy had worked. "Let's catch us some wild Injuns," he said, and wheeled the cayuse around. Putting his heels to its flanks, he rode to rescue the woman he'd been hired to find.

The trail, so freshly made, was easy to follow. Already the Navahos were specks in the distance, and they were still riding hard. He knew he must not get too close or they might spot him, and he wanted the element of surprise on his side when he made his bid to free Gretchen.

The stallion didn't seem affected by the heat, leading Fargo to conclude that it had drunk recently. The Navahos might know of secret watering holes, since their tribe had been crisscrossing the Jornada del Muerto for generations. Such knowledge would be jealously guarded, forbidden to whites and other tribes alike.

In all directions the countryside was flat and bleak. Fargo was glad the Jornada del Muerto contained few stretches of sand dunes such as were found in the desert country much farther west. Horses tended to bog down in heavy sand and wore themselves out just staying upright.

The time crept along.

Fargo was surprised the Navahos were abroad during the day. They knew how harsh and unyielding the desert was, knew it better than anyone, which was why they ordinarily traveled at night. He speculated that the warrior who'd escaped the previous night had led the others back.

An hour later Fargo felt sticky all over. He hadn't sweated so much in a coon's age. The Navahos were vague dots to the north, and they showed no sign of deviating from their course. If they kept going far enough, they'd eventually come to Adobe Wells. His instincts told him they would turn one way or the other long before then.

They did.

The afternoon was half over when he saw the band angle to the west. Coincidentally, a string of five mesas rose up out of nowhere to become silhouetted against the horizon. He figured the Navahos were making for those mesas. But why?

Another hour later he lost the band when they rode around the center mesa. He studied its craggy heights, concerned they had a sentry posted. When he reached it, he hugged the bottom, where there were plenty of boulders and gullies to use as cover. The tracks of the Navahos were clear as could be.

Fargo rode slowly, the plains rifle resting on his thighs, a thumb on the hammer and a finger on the trigger. A shadow suddenly flitted over him, and he glanced sharply skyward, surprised to spy a lone turkey vulture soaring high above him. Of all the big birds, vultures were found virtually everywhere. Few hawks and eagles frequented the desert, because game was so scarce. But vultures, existing on carrion, found enough to eat in any kind of terrain. This one flew in a circle, regarding Fargo for a minute, and then gave a lethargic flap of its big black wings to send it up and over the top of the mesa.

He hoped the Navahos hadn't seen the bird. They might wonder about what it had been eyeing and send a warrior to investigate. He came to a square block of stone twice the size of his mount and halted at the far corner to peer at the land ahead.

The Navahos were half a mile away, approaching a butte, a smaller version of a mesa. Curling up from the center of the butte was a thin column of smoke.

Fargo had found their camp. He pondered whether to cross the open space between the mesa and the butte right then or to wait for nightfall, and decided on the latter. Doing so now would invite discovery, and he figured Gretchen was safe for the time being, as safe as she could be under the circumstances. Dismounting, he retained a hold on the reins and walked around the block until he was in its shadow.

He sat down, the rifle in the same hand as the reins, braced his back against the stone, and wearily closed his eyes. What he wouldn't give for a few hours' sleep! He was tuckered out through and through. Every muscle felt sore. When he got back to Albuquerque he might spend a week in bed just for the hell of it. A little female company wouldn't hurt matters none, neither.

His mind began to drift, and suddenly Fargo realized he was dozing off. Exercising supreme will power, he brought himself around. For the moment. But how was he to stay awake until nightfall, which was three or four hours off? He pinched his cheek until it hurt, but the pain failed to invigorate his flagging body.

He thought of the Ovaro and hoped the pinto was safe. That horse and him went back a long ways, and he'd grown attached to the critter over the years. Of all the horses he'd owned, the Ovaro had suited him best. He didn't like to think he wouldn't see it again.

Next he dwelled on Delgado's bunch. He couldn't wait to track them down and repay them in kind for what they had done to him. And if they'd already sold the Ovaro, he'd make them pay double.

The cayuse fidgeted and tried to walk off in the direction of the butte.

"No, you don't," Fargo said, tightening his grip on the reins. The horse fidgeted some more, so he put his left hand on the ground, about to rise and calm it down. That was when he felt something crawl onto the back of his hand, something big, something that stopped and brushed the tops of his knuckles. He looked down and was horrified to see a giant desert hairy scorpion.

18

Everything that Fargo knew about scorpions flashed through his mind. They ate spiders and other large insects and preferred to do their hunting in the cool of the night. During the day they stayed under rocks or in any handy shaded areas. They used their wicked poisonous stingers to kill their prey, and some scorpions had poison that could kill humans quicker than rattler venom. Others weren't quite as deadly, although their sting was excruciatingly painful and would cause their victim's afflicted flesh to swell up like a bloated corpse. They weren't aggressive toward people, but they would sting when deliberately provoked or accidentally disturbed.

The large specimen resting on Fargo's hand was nearly six inches long. Its poison wasn't lethal, but it would render his arm useless for a spell and make him sicker than a dog. The creature's back was black; its ugly head, eight arched legs, twin pincers, and tail were all yellow. The stinger itself was black. Short, dark hair grew on its legs and stomach, which accounted for its peculiar name.

Fargo suppressed an impulse to lift his hand and fling the scorpion away. The movement might goad it to attack. He waited instead, knowing that eventually it would amble on. Unfortunately, the scorpion didn't appear to be in any hurry. It stood there, its pincers waving slightly, its mouth opening and closing as if it was chewing.

Fargo figured he could outlast the critter. Sweat beaded his brow and trickled down his spine, but he ignored it. So long as he didn't budge, he'd be fine.

Suddenly the cayuse tried to take a step, jerking on the reins as it bobbed its head.

Caught unaware, Fargo was nearly pulled off balance. He bunched his arm muscles and held tight. The stallion lifted its head again, tugging hard, and Fargo's entire body quivered from the strain of resisting the pull. He glared at the horse, irate. It had picked a hell of a time to act up.

The scorpion's multiple legs moved and it crawled over an inch, then halted directly on top of Fargo's fingers.

He could feel the tiny barbs in the scorpion's feet digging into his skin. One of the pincers scraped his little finger and he inadvertently flinched. He thought he might be able to tilt his hand a mite and the creature would take the hint and walk off. But when he started to elevate his palm, the scorpion's tail uncoiled.

He watched the stinger, ready to whip his hand out should that poisonous black needle abruptly swoop down. The scorpion shifted positions and faced the horse, perhaps trying to figure out what in the world the four-legged animal was. Fargo firmed his grip on the reins to prevent the cayuse from acting up again.

After an interval that seemed like an eternity to Fargo, the scorpion walked off his finger and strolled along the base of the huge block of stone. Good riddance, he reflected, and stood. He should have known better than to sit down without first taking a gander at the ground where he was going to plant his posterior. His fatigue was making him increasingly careless.

He stepped to the end of the block and studied the butte. The smoke continued to climb lazily upward. There were no Navahos to be seen, but he was sure they had a sentry posted. If he tried to cross the clear tract ringing the butte, they'd know about it and prepare a suitable reception.

Frowning, he leaned back against the stone and resigned himself to the long wait until nightfall. The heat was nearly unbearable, even in the shade, and several times during the next few hours he mopped his brow and lifted his shirt to let the warm air cool his sweat-slick chest and stomach.

His thoughts rambled, from Grace to Gretchen to the Shakers, and to his plans for the future after he got his revenge on the Delgado outfit. He contemplated moseying north, maybe high up into the central Rockies, where there was still a mantle of snow and delightfully cold temperatures. The idea appealed to him even more than a week at a hotel and the companionship of a willing filly.

The shadows were lengthening when Fargo finally roused himself and straightened. He moved around his shelter and saw that the sun was halfway below the western horizon. Darkness wouldn't fall for a while yet.

Maybe he wouldn't wait until then. He glanced at the cayuse, an idea bubbling in his brain. A little light to see by would increase his odds. Since he could ride as well as any Indian who ever lived, the trick he had in mind should enable him to reach the butt undetected.

The sun eased lower. The shadows grew longer and longer.

When only a fiery crescent remained, Fargo mounted. He transferred the plains rifle to his left hand, hooked his left elbow around the horse's neck, and eased himself down until he was flush with the animal's ribs and belly, his left leg resting on its back. He clamped his right leg underneath the cayuse. Unless someone was up close, they'd have no idea the horse carried a rider. Indians were notorious for swinging over the sides of their mounts during a battle and unleashing arrows from under the necks of their steeds.

He dug his left heel into the horse and the cayuse moved out from behind the stone block, making straight for the butte. Peeking out under the animal's jaw, Fargo scoured the face of the flat-topped hill. From the way the cayuse had been behaving, he figured it had been there several times before and probably associated the butte with food, water, and rest.

A glimmer of light became visible halfway there, at the base of the butte near the middle.

The stallion plodded on unerringly toward the light, walking faster the closer it got. Fargo noticed an odd quality to the campfire. The flames danced and writhed as they should, but their outline was blurred and the colors were paler than they should be.

When he was only thirty yards from the butte, the reason became obvious. Fargo realized there was a cleft running down the center from top to bottom, a gap wide enough to admit a horse, and the fire actually blazed in the recesses of that cleft. The light he saw shimmering so vaguely was a reflection.

Fargo was within twenty yards of the opening when he saw a shadowy figure glide in front of the reflection. Instantly, he lowered himself to the ground and lay flat on his stomach. The cayuse kept going. He observed the shadow detach itself from the butte and come out to fetch the animal. A low voice spoke in Navaho tongue.

Fargo stayed put until the sentry had hold of the horse and was leading it back into the cleft. Then he slowly rose into a crouch and trailed the brave. His plan had worked just dandy so far.

He halted at the cleft, standing to one side, and watched the forms of the bulky horse and the lean warrior proceed over thirty feet. The fire was beyond them, revealing both man and animal in inky silhouette. Keeping low and near the left-hand wall, Fargo crept into the cleft and advanced until he was close to the opposite end. Loud voices prompted him to squat and slide forward on his soles until he could see the entire camp.

The setup impressed him. Erosion had long since worn out the center of the butte, forming a natural bowl surrounded by high walls, an ideal spot for a hideout or camp. The fire crackled in the middle of the bowl, beside the glimmering surface of a spring. There was grass for forage and a few bushes. And as near as Fargo could tell, there was only the one way in or out.

He flattened and crawled out of the gap, bearing to his left, his elbow brushing the wall. The Navahos were to the right of the fire. Most had stood, including his old acquaintance Spotted Horse, when the sentry brought the cayuse up, and they were now examining the horse and conversing excitedly, evidently about the warrior who had owned it.

Where the hell was Gretchen?

Fargo's path became blocked by a patch of high grass, into which he crawled and stopped so he could scour the camp for the woman. If he'd miscalculated, if any harm had come to her, he'd never be able to forgive himself. There were horses tethered to the right of the Navahos, a long line of sixteen animals standing partially in the shadows, only their rumps basking in the glow from the campfire.

Where had the extra horses come from? Fargo wondered. There had been seven earlier. Even adding the four mounts belonging to the quartet he'd tangled with the previous night, there were still five too many.

He spied packs and bundles lying near the horses. Since Indians knew how to live off the land and never carried burdensome supplies when on a raid, he was at a loss to explain their presence. Something moved near the packs, and his eyes narrowed when he saw someone sit up and gaze at the Navahos. Golden hair caught the firelight nicely.

Gretchen!

Fargo crawled onward, fixing to make a complete circuit of the bowl and approach Gretchen from the rear. It would put the string of horses between him and the Navahos, and if none of the animals gave him away, he might be able to sneak her off once the warriors fell asleep. He froze when the sentry headed for the gap and another warrior added the cayuse to the string. Once the Navahos were settled down and talking, he resumed his circuit.

Then someone groaned loudly.

Stopping, Fargo listened to the groan go on and on. It was coming from near the horses, but he couldn't pinpoint the exact spot. A tall warrior rose, walked over to the right of where the horses stood, and was momentarily out of Fargo's view, screened by the animals. He heard sharp words in Navaho, then a slap and a laugh. The tall warrior, the same one who had abducted Gretchen, reappeared. He walked up to her and said something, then returned to his fellow braves.

Perplexed, Fargo snaked around the bowl. The Navahos must have another prisoner, he concluded, but who? The rest of the Shakers were dead. Maybe it was one of the four Shaker women taken from the wagon train, or possibly all four. He would have thought the Navahos would get the women to their village pronto, but maybe they hadn't.

The Navahos were having a grand time. They talked and laughed and munched on roasted lizard. Despite the loss of so many of their friends, they had counted many corpses and taken captives. They would be hailed as brave men by their entire tribe when they got back.

The sight and scent of the lizard made Fargo's stomach growl. He recollected fondly the snake he'd never gotten to eat and yearned for a morsel of food to appease his appetite. It was too bad that scorpion hadn't been another rattler. Chasing all thoughts of food from his head, he crawled and crawled, the rifle clutched in both hands, his elbows bent, his knees bearing most of his weight. By the time he'd gone three-fourths of the way around, his legs ached from his thighs to his toes.

Stars glinted in the heavens. The cool night breeze found its way over the high walls and fanned the writhing flames.

Fargo exercised greater caution as he approached the horses. The snort of a single startled animal would alert the warriors. He noticed that one of the horses was considerably bigger than most of the others and was standing near the end of the string nearest him. The animal was the first to swing its head directly at him, leaving no doubt that it had seen him. Apparently unconcerned, it didn't utter a sound.

The horse at the very end of the string was the second one to see him. Fargo couldn't tell much about it because its features, like those of the big animal beside it, were shrouded in shadows. This horse tried to take a step in his direction but was stopped by the tether.

He could see Gretchen, the picture of despair, seated with her face buried in her arms and her shoulders trembling as she cried silently. Her wrists were bound. Pausing, he grabbed the Arkansas toothpick and tried not to think of what would happen if the Navahos should discover him now.

The groaner started up again.

Fargo waited to see if the tall warrior or another would walk over to shut the person up. From the low tone, he was convinced the groaner must be a man. Had the Navahos captured an Apache? Or was it some poor prospector whose lust for gold had gotten him into more trouble than he'd bargained on? The mournful sound ceased, and Fargo crawled to within two yards of the horses. Gretchen was not fifteen feet away, her back toward him. Since he couldn't attempt to rescue her yet, he forced himself to relax, his chin resting on his right wrist. Out of the corner of his eye he saw that the two horses on the end, their eyes barely visible in the gloom, were staring hard at him. There was something familiar about the pair, and he wished there was enough light to see them clearly.

On a whim Fargo moved closer to them. It took a moment for his eyes to register the white patches on the big horse, and then with a start he recognized the animal; it was the Ovaro! And the smaller one next to the pinto was the pack animal he'd bought back in Albuquerque. In his surprise he began to rise, but stopped himself in time. Easing forward until he was in front of the string, he crouched and reached up to pet his stallion. The bay demanded attention too. As he stroked them he heard another low moan and concluded it must be one of Delgado's outfit or Delgado himself. They hadn't made it out of the Jornada del Muerto, and he didn't feel sorry for them in the least. But he did wonder about his guns. Did the Navahos have them? If he could get his hands on the Colt and the Sharps, escaping would be a damn sight easier.

He rubbed the Ovaro's neck, then moved slowly along the line, curious to learn the identity of the other prisoner. Loud voices sounded, and he rose up high enough to see over the animals.

Spotted Horse and the tall warrior were walking toward the horses.

19

Fargo stopped and hunkered down, peering between two of the horses to watch the braves approach. They were gabbing like two squaws at a lodge raising and gave no indication that they knew he was there. On the way past Gretchen the tall Navaho lashed out with his foot, striking her in the shoulder and knocking her over. Both warriors laughed at her distress.

The pair halted at the packs and bundles. Spotted Horse rummaged around, then straightened with a rifle in his hand.

Even in the dim light the size and shape of the rifle were distinctive. Fargo immediately recognized it as a Sharps and surmised it must be his own. He saw the two Indians pick up other guns and discuss them, leading him to conclude all of the weapons taken from Delgado's bunch had been piled there until the warriors got around to dividing them. If he could only reach them!

After a few minutes of animated discussion the two Navahos went back to the fire. The tall warrior had stuck a hogleg in the top of his pants and kept patting the butt affectionately, delighted with his new weapon.

Fargo wondered why the Navahos hadn't had the guns with them during the fight at the ravine. He guessed it was because they were accustomed to using their traditional weapons and needed time to practice with the firearms before they would be proficient enough to justify using a gun in battle. Then, too, many Indians preferred bows and arrows over rifles and pistols, and with good reason. A skilled warrior could shoot arrows as rapidly as a rifleman could fire a long gun and with equal or better accuracy.

He continued to the end of the string and knelt. The horses regarded him with interest, but none expressed alarm. Lying close by, tied spread-eagled on the ground, was a naked man neither moving nor uttering any sounds. Fargo edged nearer until the man's features became clear enough to identify.

It was Felipe.

The Navahos had done terrible things to the fledgling hardcase, the sort of things that made grown women faint and children become violently ill. Fargo had seen such gruesome handiwork before and merely scowled.

A lifetime spent around Indians had taught him that in most respects they were no better or worse than whites. The savage acts they frequently committed weren't the result of an innately cruel character. Rather, Indians lived a life of violence from their cradleboards to their dying breaths. Whether they were hunting, raiding, or simply defending their villages, Indians were constantly put upon to kill or be killed. Such a harsh life hardened them to where they viewed pain and suffering as part of the natural order of things and entertained no qualms about treating their enemies as life often treated them.

Fargo moved over to Felipe and leaned forward. Felipe's eyes were open, dark pools of agonized torment, and they blinked as Fargo's face materialized above them. The pink tip of a tongue flicked out and wetted Felipe's parched, cracked lips.

"You," he croaked, the word barely audible.

"Where are your *compañeros*?" Fargo whispered, casting a glance at the Navahos.

"Dead. All dead," Felipe said, his lips hardly moving.

Fargo didn't know whether to be happy or mad. The Navahos had deprived him of his revenge. He'd wanted to pay Delgado back, to give the bastard a taste of his own medicine. "How long have you been here?"

"Lost track."

"It wouldn't help much if I was to cut you loose," Fargo said, staring at the man's private parts. Or what was left of them. "I wish there was something I could do."

"There is," Felipe said softly.

"What?" Fargo asked, knowing the answer.

"Kill me."

Fargo looked at the warriors again, his hand tightening on the hilt of the throwing knife.

"*Por favor,*" Felipe begged. "I know we have been

enemies." He paused to take a breath, and a deep hole in the side of his chest made a sucking noise. "But no man deserves this."

Fargo placed the rifle on the ground.

"Please. Even hombres like us have honor, eh?"

Fargo nodded. Then, without warning, he placed his left hand over Felipe's mouth to prevent him from crying out even as he speared the knife into the man's chest, the long blade entering at just the right angle to pierce the heart. Felipe's eyes went wide, his back arched, and he gurgled, or tried to. Fargo felt spittle on his palm, felt Felipe's mouth moving, until suddenly the young tough went limp. Fargo kept his hand over Felipe's mouth for ten seconds more to be sure, then wiped his palm on his buckskins.

Gripping the plains rifle, Fargo flattened again and crawled toward the packs and bundles. They shielded him from the Navahos, and he was able to get right up behind them without being spotted. The glow from the fire bathed the ground around him in a dim light, and he had to be careful lest any motion alert them to the fact that they had an unexpected visitor at their hideaway. Off to the right, Gretchen once again sat with her face buried in her arms, sniffling.

The weapons were lying in front of the packs. To grab them he must slide an arm into the open. He considered crawling back beyond the horses and waiting until the Navahos slept, but he risked having some of the other warriors help themselves to his guns before he got his hands on them. He couldn't let that happen.

Fargo slid the Arkansas toothpick into its sheath, raised an eye above the closest pack so he could watch the braves, and slowly extended his right arm between the pack and another one. When his arm was at full extension, his fingers were at the edge of the pile of weapons. The Sharps lay four or five inches from the tips of his fingertips. He didn't see the Colt.

A hefty warrior abruptly stood, a tomahawk in his left hand, and came toward the horses.

Fargo had nowhere to go, nowhere to hide. In a few more strides the brave would see him and shout a warning. He had to hope the Sharps and the other guns were loaded; otherwise

Felipe wouldn't be the only one serving as buzzard bait. At the very bottom of the pile lay the ammunition for the various arms. He would have no time to reload the Sharps. Once he fired, he must grab one of the revolvers and cut loose.

Gretchen heard the warrior coming and looked up.

The Navaho gazed at her and grinned lecherously.

Relying on the distraction to slow the warrior's reflexes for a fraction of a second, Fargo clutched the Sharps and surged to his knees. He pressed the stock against his shoulder, cocked the powerful rifle, and fired as the heavy Navaho faced him in blatant astonishment. The slug ripped into the warrior's abdomen and bowled him over.

Instantly, the remaining six Navahos were on their feet and taking in the situation at a glance. The tall brave clawed at the gun he'd appropriated. Two others charged, each bringing a knife into play. Spotted Horse ran for the gap.

Fargo's Colt was lying in plain view now. The revolver had been hidden under the Sharps. He saw it as he let go of the rifle and lunged forward over the pack, and he promptly palmed the .44 and straightened. His thumb stroked the hammer twice in swift succession, and the onrushing Navahos were sent sprawling.

The tall warrior had unlimbered his pistol and pointed it at Fargo. He had tried to fire it by squeezing the trigger, but nothing happened. He didn't know enough about revolvers to realize he held a single-action; to shoot it, the hammer first had to be pulled all the way back, and then the trigger could be squeezed.

Fargo saw the brave's mistake and dispatched him with a shot to the head. In the opening seconds of the fight he'd killed four of the seven warriors. Spotted Horse had safely reached the cleft, and the other two warriors were hard on his heels.

An awful silence descended on the butte.

Stepping over the packs, Fargo squatted and searched for his gunbelt. He found it and quickly replaced the spent cartridges, his eyes darting every which way. Gretchen gaped at him in amazement. The horses were gazing over their shoulders at him, the majority unruffled by the gunplay because they were war horses accustomed to loud noises and brutal battles. Delgado's animals, though, fidgeted fearfully. There was no activity at the cleft, but three of the band were still alive and would retaliate in some way. He fed in the last cartridge and stood.

"Skye?" Gretchen said in disbelief, and then sobbed. "Oh, Skye! I thought you were dead." She stood and ran toward him, tears lining her eyes.

Fargo motioned with his left hand, stopping her in her tracks. He needed a clear view of the bowl in case the Navahos burst out of the cleft.

"What—" Gretchen began, then looked at the gap. "Oh."

"Hold out your arms," Fargo directed, stepping over to her and drawing the toothpick. He stood so he could see the gap and sawed at the rope binding her wrists until she was freed. "There."

"What do we do now?" Gretchen asked, rubbing the marks where the rope had bit into her skin.

"We skedaddle," Fargo said. "Those Injuns will take a while to decide how they want to come at us. I wouldn't put it past them to try and climb the butte to gain the high ground."

"Perhaps they'll leave without a fight. They've seen what you can do."

Fargo jerked a thumb at the string. "They won't go anywhere without their horses, and the only way to get them is through us." He glanced at the packs and bundles. "Did you happen to see any saddles around here?"

"No. Sure didn't."

It figures, Fargo reflected. Indian men were trained from childhood to ride bareback. As adults they sometimes used small saddles constructed from leather and stuffed with grass or buffalo hair. But they had a definite disdain for the type of saddles used by the whites and the Mexicans. Indians believed only inferior riders would use such outlandish affairs. Fargo imagined that his saddle and those belonging to Delgado's outfit were lying out in the desert, tossed aside by the contemptuous Navahos. What a waste. "Ever ridden bareback?"

"When I was a little girl," Gretchen answered. "I can do it again if need be."

"Untie the pinto and the bay at the west end of the string," Fargo instructed her. "The bay is yours."

She nodded and hurried to the horses.

Fargo picked up the Sharps and ran to the cleft. Being careful not to expose himself, he peeked along its dim, empty length. Spotted Horse and the other two were out there somewhere, plotting to kill Gretchen and him. If they were smart, they'd guess his next move and wait at the entrance. He had to hope their thirst for vengeance would cause them to overlook the obvious.

He sprinted back to where Gretchen was holding the reins to the Ovaro and the bay. "We've got to make our break now. Are you up to it?"

"I'll do my best," she said. "But why not wait until daylight? We can see them then."

"And they can see us," Fargo pointed out. "No, we go now. They might not be expecting us to try so soon, and we might be able to surprise them."

"Might," Gretchen said.

"Can you handle a gun?"

"I've never fired a shot in my life."

"Forget the idea. You'd be so busy trying to shoot that they'd nail you for certain." Fargo nodded at the bay. "Get aboard."

Gretchen mounted fluidly and squared her slender shoulders. "I'm ready when you are." She smiled down at him. "And before we go, I want to thank you from the bottom of my heart for rescuing me. For a while there I expected to wind up my days on earth as a white squaw."

"We're not safe yet," Fargo reminded her. "Keep watch on that opening," he said, and stepped to the packs and bundles. He found his saddlebags right off and slung them over his left shoulder. A bit of searching turned up an empty water bag. Hastening to the spring, he filled it and returned.

"Are we ready?" Gretchen asked anxiously.

"Not quite," Fargo said. He handed the water bag to her, then went to the string and untied every horse. A sorrel moved a few yards, but the rest stood still. He walked to the fire and was about to kick it out when an idea struck him. Working rapidly, he took every weapon he could find and dumped the whole lot into the spring, even the bows and lances belonging to the Navahos. After the last lance splashed into the depths, he extinguished the fire, and darkness enveloped the bowl like a black cloud.

"Skye?" Gretchen said.

"Right here," Fargo assured her, stepping to her side. "Give me the water bag."

"I can manage. You'll have your hands full as it is."

She was right, so Fargo didn't argue. He climbed onto the Ovaro, glad to have the reliable stallion under him again. "Stay behind me every step of the way," he continued.

"I can barely see you, but I'll try."

"Once we're in the clear I'll cut to the north," Fargo explained, thinking the information would make it easier for her.

"Which direction is north?"

"Just stay close," Fargo stressed, and rode to the west end of the line of horses. Gretchen trailed him. He reached out to touch her shoulder. "Get set."

"I'm ready."

Smiling grimly, Fargo drew the Colt. With the reins and the Sharps in one hand and the .44 in the other, he commenced hollering and flapping his arms. The horses belonging to Delgado's outfit bolted toward the opening, and the war horses joined them in the exodus. He screeched to goad them on, then followed the last animal into the cleft at a canter. Everything now depended on where the three Navahos were. If they were scaling the butte, Gretchen and he would easily make their getaway. He strained to see the entrance through the dust raised by the horses, and he was almost there when he spied a brave with a bow just outside.

20

The Navaho spotted Fargo, raised the bow, and started to pull back the string.

Fargo snapped off two shots in the blink of an eye and saw the warrior spin and fall. Then he was out of the cleft and cutting to the left, sitting upright instead of hunching over the pinto to draw attention to himself and not Gretchen. It was a foolish risk, but he'd do whatever was necessary to protect her from harm. He expected to get an arrow or a knife in the back, and the skin between his shoulder blades prickled as if from a heat rash. He didn't see Spotted Horse or the last buck anywhere near the gap, so he twisted and scanned the face of the butte. It was well he did, for perched on a narrow ledge fifteen feet up was one of the Navahos, his features obscured by the gloom. Steel glinted dully, and Fargo pointed the Colt over his right shoulder and fired once.

The warrior screamed, swayed, and pitched headfirst from the ledge to thud onto the ground behind the bay.

Now only one remained.

Fargo never let the Ovaro break its stride. Gretchen was riding almost on its tail, smartly bending her body flush with the bay's back. He faced front, about to drive his heels into the pinto's sides in order to get it to go faster, when he glimpsed a rushing figure charge at him from out of the night on his right. Before he could turn to bring the Colt to bear, the figure launched itself into the air and Fargo felt steely arms encircle his waist as he was swept from the Ovaro. The Sharps went flying. He shifted, trying to flip his attacker underneath him so the warrior would take the brunt of the impact, but the brave adroitly checked the motion by shifting in the opposite direction, and they both slammed down on their sides. Fargo hit on his gun arm, his elbow smashing into the earth, and his entire arm went numb.

For a second he was face-to-face with his foe. It was Spotted Horse.

Then the Navaho shoved loose and pushed to his feet, a long knife gripped in his right hand, his features contorted in a snarl.

Fargo was nearly as quick. He rose and stepped backward, retaining his grip on the .44 but unable to lift his arm to shoot. His arm hung limply from the elbow down.

Spotted Horse noticed and smirked. "Now you die, white eyes," he hissed, and swung viciously.

Sliding to the right, Fargo avoided the first blow. He had to backpedal as Spotted Horse pressed his advantage, swinging over and over, and each time the tip of the blade came a bit closer to Fargo's torso. Once the point tugged at his shirt and he felt the buckskin rip.

Tingling in Fargo's arm told him that he would soon have use of his hand. The streaking knife prevented him from trying a border shift or from grabbing for the toothpick. All he could do was continue to backpedal and wait. Suddenly Spotted Horse employed a new tactic. The Navaho began a swing at Fargo's chest, then turned the motion into a straight stab at Fargo's left thigh. In pure reflex Fargo pivoted, felt the blade nick his pants, and smacked the Colt into the warrior's mouth. His arm was better!

Spotted Horse seemed unfazed by the blow, and as Fargo's arm dropped away the Navaho lunged with his free hand, grasping Fargo's wrist, and speared his knife at Fargo's neck.

Jerking his head to one side, Fargo bought himself a few more moments of life. He clamped his free hand on Spotted Horse's wrist to keep the brave from using the knife again, and for several seconds they strained in each other's grasp, each striving to wrench his arm free, to use his weapon. The Navaho was strong, but Fargo was stronger, and slowly his strength prevailed. He felt his right wrist begin to slip out of Spotted Horse's hold. One swift shot and the fight would be over.

The Navaho realized the same thing. He abruptly whipped his right leg into Fargo's right knee and Fargo's leg buckled. Without mercy Spotted Horse kicked at the other knee, but Fargo evaded his foot.

To take the warrior off-guard, Fargo dropped into a squat

and instantly uncoiled both legs, driving his shoulder into the Navaho's midsection. Breath whooshed from Spotted Horse and the man doubled over. Fargo lashed his head up and back and winced when his cranium delivered a smashing blow to the brave's mouth. The grip on his wrist slackened.

Straightening, Fargo drove his knee into the Navaho's groin and heard Spotted Horse grunt in pain. He tore his right hand free, jammed the barrel into the warrior's sternum, and fired. Muffled by the pressure, the Colt still bucked as the slug bored through Spotted Horse's chest.

Hurled backward by the blast, Spotted Horse tottered on his heels and then fell on his back. The knife slipped to the ground. He attempted to rise, to lift himself on his elbow, but was too weak to do it. Gasping, he fell back down and blinked up at the sky.

Fargo stepped up to the Navaho, cocked the .44, and trained the barrel on his adversary's forehead. "This is for all the Shakers," he said.

In a final act of defiance Spotted Horse lifted his head and hissed in English, "Go to hell, bastard."

"You first," Fargo said. He stroked the trigger, the revolver spouted flames and lead, and a dark dot sprouted in the center of the Indian's brow. Fargo slowly lowered the gun, feeling weariness pervade every inch of his body. It was over. There was still the ride to Adobe Wells, but the war party had finally been disposed of. He began reloading the Colt.

"Are you all right, Skye?"

Fargo turned, surprised to find Gretchen astride the bay not ten feet away. "You should have kept on riding," he admonished her.

"I couldn't leave you."

"You're some gal. You've got enough grit for three women."

"It's easy to be brave when you're around someone who is braver."

The affection and gratitude in her voice touched Fargo. He slid the .44 into its holster, found the Sharps, and looked around for the Ovaro, which had halted ten yards off and was waiting for him. Most horses would have spooked and been a mile away by now. It made him appreciate how lucky he was to have the critter back. He strode to the pinto and swung up. "If we push it, we can be at Adobe Wells by tomorrow afternoon. Are you up to it?"

Her teeth flashed in the night. "Make any sudden stops and I'll ride right over you."

"Then let's hit the trail," Fargo said, and turned his back on the butte and the dead Navahos without another thought. The other horses had scattered in all directions and were no longer in sight. He believed he spied one or two off in the distance during the next hour, but they didn't come close enough to confirm it. The Indian war horses would manage quite well, he figured, and might even find their way back to the Navaho village. Delgado's animals didn't know the lay of the land, but somewhere in the remote annals of their ancestry had lived the original wild stock from which they sprang, and those latent instincts would now serve them in good stead.

During the hours until dawn Fargo was preoccupied with one goal: getting the hell out of the Jornada del Muerto as rapidly as possible. Until the sun rose he pushed the Ovaro to its limit and was glad the feisty bay kept up. Once the fiery orb dominated the blue sky, he slowed a mite. Frequently he stopped to let the horses drink water from his cupped palms and to give some to Gretchen. He drank sparingly in case something went wrong and they should need the water even more later on.

The prospect of bidding adios to the hostile desert made the morning and early afternoon hours pass swiftly. Fargo constantly surveyed the north horizon for the change in the landscape that would tell him they were almost to the Los Pinos Mountains. When, at midafternoon, he spotted a few small humps so far off that they resembled anthills, he assumed the heat was deceiving his eyes. After riding another mile and seeing the humps grow slightly, he realized they were the mountains he sought and allowed himself the luxury of a congratulatory smile.

Gretchen didn't spot them until another mile was behind them. "Are they what I think they are?" she asked excitedly.

"Yep. We'll be spending the night at Adobe Wells. Tomorrow morning we head for Albuquerque and your sister."

The horses seemed to sense that the end of their arduous desert journey was at hand. They both broke into a gallop without any urging.

Two hours later the ruins of Adobe Wells appeared and beckoned invitingly. Fargo didn't let his enthusiasm get the better of him. He cradled the Sharps and alertly scanned the countryside for sign of hostiles and the ground for fresh tracks. There were none of either, leading him to deduce that no one had been there since Delgado's bunch ambushed him.

He angled past the old mission and went straight to the spring. Both the Ovaro and the bay rode up to the water's edge and greedily plunged their mouths into the cool liquid. Gretchen was a step behind them, dropping to her hands and knees and gulping lustily.

Fargo took his time. He checked the land around them, then the soil near the spring. There were abundant small animal tracks but no human prints. Satisfied they were safe, he slid down, leaned the rifle on a large rock, and knelt beside the spring. He cupped water to his mouth while observing Gretchen drink faster than the horses. "Take your time," he cautioned. "Drink too fast and you'll wind up with an ache in your belly."

"But I'm so hot!"

"The spring isn't going anywhere," Fargo noted.

Gretchen stood and stared at the surface, a gleam in her eyes. "I have a better idea," she said.

"What?"

She gazed right and left, then at him, her brow furrowed. Then she tentatively began unfastening the buttons on her dress. She gained confidence with each button and had her breasts partly exposed before Fargo blurted out a question.

"What in tarnation are you doing?"

"I want to take a dip, to feel that wonderful water all over my body, and I don't care if it's a shameless thing to do."

"I don't know," Fargo said uncertainly.

"Will I pollute the spring?" Gretchen inquired while undoing the last of the buttons.

"No, I reckon you won't."

"Then let's do it."

"Both of us?" Fargo said. While the notion appealed to him,

he didn't like the idea of standing around naked when there was a remote chance Indians might show up.

"Sure," Gretchen said, smiling. She was stripping with an expertise that would have made a saloon girl jealous. "Come on. Just for a few minutes. You know you want to."

The sight of her firm breasts and tight tummy stirred Fargo's manhood. He should be thinking about finding them something to eat, not sex. But the riveting sight of a lovely woman in the altogether was enough to replace any man's appetite for food with another appetite entirely. He searched the area, saw nothing moving, and shucked his gunbelt and buckskins.

Gretchen had her toes in the water and was giggling while wriggling them playfully. "How deep is this spring?"

"I don't rightly know."

"Well, I can't swim. Will you hold me while I step out?" Gretchen requested, and extended her left arm.

Fargo stepped closer and took her hand. Her palm was hot to his touch and there was a scarlet tinge on her cheeks. She gingerly edged into the water, her eyes averted, too embarrassed to face him squarely. He held tightly to her fingers, watching the water glide up over her knees, her thighs, and her backside to her waist.

"Oh, this is delicious!" Gretchen declared. She turned and motioned with her free hand. "It's not very deep at this spot. Join me."

Feeling his manhood surge to its full length, Fargo entered the spring and moved nearer to her until the tips of her hard nipples were brushing his broad chest.

Gretchen looked down. "Oh, my," she said.

"Just remember you started this," Fargo growled, and took her into his arms. She offered no resistance, her lips hungrily leaping to meet his, her slick tongue jutting into his mouth. He brought his right hand up to caress her breast and felt her grind her hips against him. He realized that she wanted him as much as he wanted her, which stoked his passion into an inferno.

They ran their hands over one another in uninhibited abandon. Gretchen seemed to have lost all her reserve. She even lowered her left hand to his organ and gently wrapped her fingers around the smooth shaft.

Fargo's loins constricted and he felt as if he might explode before he wanted. Palming her other pert breast, he rubbed and tweaked them both until they hung heavy and ripe. His tongue licked her neck, throat, and shoulders. Where before he hadn't had enough saliva to make spit, he now had enough to quench a forest fire.

They kissed and fondled until they were both breathing heavier than the horses, their bodies vibrant with keen desire. Fargo slowly backed from the water, and once they had firm ground under their feet he scooped her into his arms and deposited her on top of his discarded clothes.

Gretchen cooed and opened her arms and legs to receive him. "You can't imagine how much I want you," she said huskily. "Ever since that time in the cliff dwelling. I can't get enough."

"Far be it from me to disappoint a lady," Fargo said, grinning, and sank to his knees. He ran his hands along her tender inner thighs, feeling her muscles twitch, and touched a hand to her nether mound. She quivered and crossed her arms over her chest, causing her breasts to bulge. The top of her tongue protruded between her rosy lips.

Fargo inserted a finger into her moist tunnel and she squirmed and panted.

"Oh, that feels so good!"

He inserted a second finger and her inner walls closed around them both. Pumping his forearms, he began a rhythmic motion that imitated a heated coupling. She responded with ardent vigor, bucking her hips to meet his hand, her knees outflung, the picture of voluptuous sensuality.

Fargo kept at it until she gripped his arms and tried to pull him down. His hand was covered with her womanly juices and her moist scent tingled his nose. He kissed her breasts, her stomach, and the soft skin above her pubic hair.

"Please! Do it now!" Gretchen pleaded.

He withdrew his fingers, positioned his organ at her trembling crack, and shoved into her like a stallion into a willing mare. She cried out, her back lifting off the ground, and sank her fingernails into his powerful biceps.

"That's it! That's it!"

Fargo stoked her furnace, their stomachs smacking together wildly. She clung to him in desperate need, and he didn't know how much longer he could contain himself. His manhood was on the verge of exploding. He pounded harder, wanting to enjoy the sensations to the hilt, and felt her insides abruptly become wetter.

"Ohhhh! Sky! It's now! It's now!"

Letting himself go, Fargo rammed into her. He spurted, filling her, his ecstasy profound, oblivious to the world. So it was that it took him a few belated seconds to react when a harsh laugh fell on his ears from directly to their rear.

"My turn next, hombre, eh?"

Struggling to control his pulsating body, Fargo gritted his teeth and glanced over his right shoulder. In all his years he had never felt so awkward, vulnerable, and stupid as he did now. In all his travels he had seldom been as astonished as he now was. Standing eight feet away, smirking in evil triumph, a pistol clutched in his right hand, was the last person in the world Fargo expected to see.

José Delgado.

21

"I heard tell that you were dead," Fargo said, keeping his voice level so Delgado wouldn't realize how flustered he truly was.

"There were many who thought so," Delgado said. "My men, the Navahos, they all gave me up as lost." He absently brushed his left hand across his sweat-stained shirt, and fine dust swirled out of the fabric. His whole appearance had taken a drastic turn for the worse. No longer was he the dashing hardcase who had confronted Fargo in Albuquerque. Now he was hatless and wore boots that had been scuffed and rubbed from constant walking until none of the original shine remained. His clothes were in no better shape. His shirt and pants were both covered with dust and torn in a half-dozen spots. Dust also caked his hair and was plastered to his face, mingled with his sweat.

Gretchen had sat up and self-consciously covered her breasts with her arms. Now she reached for the nearest garment, which happened to be Fargo's shirt.

"No you don't, señorita!" Delgado growled, moving his gun a couple of inches to train it on her. "Don't get dressed on my account. I like seeing you the way you are." He threw back his head and laughed.

Fargo, still on his knees, straightened and went to stand. But the pistol abruptly shifted toward him again.

"And I like *you* right where you are," Delgado said. "Who would ever have thought I would catch you in such a position, eh?"

"Not me," Fargo allowed, continuing to look over his shoulder at the killer. He surreptitiously glanced to his right where his gunbelt lay and estimated his chances of grabbing the Colt and getting off a shot before Delgado put a bullet in him. They were nil.

Delgado sighed and gazed at Gretchen. He licked his dry lips. "Sometimes I don't understand life at all, hombre."

Fargo knew the man loved to hear himself talk, and that weakness just might enable him to turn the tables. He had to keep Delgado gabbing away until an opening presented itself. "How do you mean?" he asked, shifting a bit, putting his right arm half an inch nearer to the .44.

"Life is so unfair," Delgado mused wryly. "*I* go into the Jornada del Muerto and barely get out alive, losing all my men and my horses in the bargain." He paused and shook his head in amazement. "*You* go into the Jornada del Muerto and not only come out alive, you bring a beautiful señorita and your stolen horses to boot." He paused again, his eyes boring into Fargo. "How did you work this miracle?"

"Luck, I reckon."

"Priests should have such luck. You should have been a man of the cloth, hombre," Delgado joked, and looked at Gretchen, ogling her voluptuous contours. "No, forget that idea. From what I just saw, you wouldn't have lasted a week as a priest." He cackled some more.

Fargo said nothing but noticed everything. The hardcase was acting oddly, was doing too much laughing at comments that weren't all that funny. He wondered if Delgado had spent a lot of time walking in the sun. The heat could do strange things to a man sometimes, could turn his mind to mush and make him behave like a little child. "How long have you been here?" he asked casually.

Delgado squinted up at the burning sun. "Two hours, no more. I had to crawl the final hundred feet or so," he said, and nodded toward the south side of the spring. "But even with my brain baking, I was smart, hombre. I crawled up to the corner of the spring near the boulder so that my tracks would not be all over out here. You would not believe how much I drank. I drank and drank until I could drink no more." He coughed. "I was afraid the Navahos were still on my trail, so I went behind the boulder and lay down in the shade. It felt so good." He stared at Fargo and snickered. "Then I heard horses and looked out, and who should it be but my old friend the Trailsman! And it isn't even my birthday, gringo."

Fargo found the information about the water extremely interesting. From personal experience he knew that anyone who drank too much after a long dry spell became heavy and sluggish. The body couldn't adjust to so much water all at once. It meant Delgado's reflexes would be slowed down considerably.

"Now what am I to do with you?" Delgado asked, more to himself than them. "I could shoot you, Fargo, and then have my way with the señorita, but that would not be as interesting, I think." He scratched the stubble on his chin. "I want to make the most of this."

"Like you made the most of killing me before by dumping me in the desert," Fargo said, and promptly regretted his foolishness.

Delgado took several quick strides forward, his eyes blazing hatred, and lashed out with the revolver.

Naked and defenseless, Fargo felt the hard barrel slam into his left temple, and he doubled over in pain. Blood flowed, and he reached up to find a nasty gash. He pressed his left hand to the wound and held his head down, trying to give the impression he was afraid of receiving another blow.

"Leave him alone!" Gretchen yelled.

"Ahh, the señorita finally talks," Delgado said sarcastically.

"Skye told me about the terrible things you did to him," Gretchen went on. "If you ask me, you're a beast and you got what you deserved when the Navahos attacked you."

Fargo expected the killer to fly into a rage and strike her. Instead, Delgado pursed his lips in thought before replying.

"Have you seen what the Navahos do to those they capture, señorita? I did. When they came at us out of nowhere, from all directions, I dived for the ground and crawled into some mesquite. From there I worked my way into a gully, then looked back. Somehow, the Navahos had missed seeing me. One of my men, Felipe, was hit in the head with a war club and fell. Later they took him away. But my other two amigos were not so lucky."

Neither Fargo nor Gretchen spoke.

"They were taken alive, although they were wounded," Delgado went on. "The savages cut out their tongues and poked

160

out their eyes. Then they peeled the skin from my friends and folded it so they could use it later in making medicine bags and such—''

"I don't want to hear any more," Gretchen interrupted.

Delgado's mouth became an evil slit. "But I insist, pretty one. I want you to know what will happen to you if the Navahos capture you."

"They already did," Gretchen blurted.

"What?"

"Skye saved me."

"Oh," Delgado said, and glanced at Fargo. "Another miracle to add to your string. I hate to admit it, *bastardo,* but everything they say about you is true." He frowned. "Oh, I heard some stories before we left Albuquerque, but I figured they were just legends."

Fargo shifted a bit more, moving his hand that much closer to the Colt.

"The Navahos must be hot on your trail," Delgado said.

A premonition made Fargo twist toward Gretchen. He wanted to signal her with his eyes so she would keep quiet, but he was too late.

"No, they're not," she stated firmly. "Skye killed all of them. He's a better man than you can ever hope to be."

Fargo bowed his head and clenched his fists, knowing the damage had been done. He received confirmation when he glanced at the hardcase and saw the sinister gleam in Delgado's eyes.

"Is that a fact, señorita?"

"It most definitely is," Gretchen said. "I was there. I saw him kill them. You could never have done half what he did."

"Who is to know?" Delgado said. "The important thing is that now I do not need to worry about the Navahos. I can concentrate on what to do with the two of you. And for this wonderful news, I thank you."

At last Gretchen perceived her mistake. She gasped and said, "Skye, I'm so sorry. I wasn't thinking."

"It's all right," Fargo said lamely, knowing damn well it wasn't all right. He slumped, and both of his hands touched the ground.

Delgado laughed. "Seeing your face, hombre, almost makes the hell I have been through worthwhile." He backed up a step. "But now we must tend to business. I want both of you to stand up."

"Why?" Gretchen asked nervously.

"What does it matter?" Delgado growled. "On your feet, woman, or I will shoot your boyfriend in the *cojones*!"

Gretchen blinked. "The what?"

"The balls, stupid one."

Fargo rose first, his arms at his sides, the image of defeat. "Why not let the woman go, Delgado?" he asked, aware he was wasting his breath. "She can't harm you."

"Don't insult me, gringo."

Gretchen was slowly standing, her arms crossed over her breasts, her thighs held close together and her hips turned sideways so the killer couldn't see her hairy thatch.

"Don't be so modest," Delgado taunted her. "After all I have seen of you, you have nothing left to hide."

"You're a brute."

The hardcase wagged the revolver to the right. "Move away from him until I tell you to stop. And hurry, or I'll shoot him."

Reluctantly, Gretchen did as she had been told. She went ten feet before the killer ordered her to halt, then she gazed sorrowfully at Fargo.

"And now we begin," Delgado said, extending his gun arm until the muzzle was within a foot of Fargo's head. "I think I will take an ear off first, then perhaps I will shoot you in the knee. What do you think?"

Fargo looked Delgado full in the eyes, the muscles on his right arm bunching. "Do I really have a choice?"

"No," Delgado said.

"Figured as much," Fargo said, and exploded into motion. He knew Delgado anticipated a desperate attempt. All he could do was hope Delgado didn't anticipate exactly what he had in mind, which was to throw himself to the left even as he flung his right arm out and hurled the contents of his right hand into Delgado's face. The dirt he had scooped into his palm struck the killer in the eyes at the very instant Delgado squeezed the trigger, and while the stinging dirt would prove no more than a temporary nuisance, it did cause Delgado to blink in the crucial moment when his finger tightened. The barrel elevated a fraction, enough to make the shot go wild and ricochet harmlessly off the enormous boulder.

Fargo landed on his shoulder and rolled, hearing the blast of the pistol again. Delgado had fired wildly into the water while trying to wipe his stinging eyes clean. He took a pace backward, the pistol sweeping from right to left.

Gretchen screamed.

Delgado swung toward her, then realized his mistake and started to swing around.

Shoving off the ground with both hands, heedless of his nudity, Fargo barreled into Delgado, his left hand clamping onto the killer's gun arm below the wrist, his right balling into a fist that he pounded into Delgado's face. Delgado tripped, bearing both of them down with Delgado on the bottom.

Fargo rained blows. He was surprised at Delgado's strength. The man absorbed his punches stoically and attempted to wrench loose. Suddenly, at the apex of one of his swings, he felt a hard object shoved against his kuckles.

"Take it!" Gretchen cried.

Without looking, Fargo opened his hand and felt the familiar contours of the .44 nestle in his palm. He cocked the hammer and pointed the barrel at Delgado, who had finally removed enough of the dirt to be able to see clearly. Delgado took one look and gulped, blanching at what he saw in Fargo's eyes.

"No!"

"Adios," Fargo said, and fired.

Just like that it was finally over. Fargo lowered the Colt and stood, hardly noticing the crimson-tinged hole in Delgado's forehead or the spreading crimson puddle under Delgado's head. He stepped to one side, grateful to be alive.

"Did I do all right?"

He turned to Gretchen. "You did just fine," he said, and she leaped into his arms and showered warm kisses on his lips.

"You saved me again," she said after a minute, her arms around his neck, her body molded to his.

"And I reckon I deserve proper thanks," Fargo responded, bending his knees so he could deposit the .44 at his feet. The friction of their bodies started his loins to twitching again.

"What do you have in mind?"

"Once more before we hit the trail."

Gretchen glanced at the dead killer. "Now? With him lying right there?"

"He won't object," Fargo said.

"I may have lived a sheltered life, but I've heard a few things," Gretchen said, grinning. "They say the word for men like you is 'kinky.' "

"Do you mind?"

"Kiss me and find out."

LOOKING FORWARD!

**The following is the opening
section from the next novel in the exciting
Trailsman series from Signet:**

THE TRAILSMAN #124
COLORADO QUARRY

*1860, just north of Pike's Peak
in the Colorado Territory, where
enterprise and killing were
too often the same thing. . . .*

He was not alone in the thickly forested hills. The big man astride the magnificent Ovaro let his lake-blue eyes scan the terrain. He'd been riding the hills for most of the day when suddenly he felt it, knew it, was sure of it. More than experience, though he certainly had enough of that. Instinct, intuition, sixth sense, premonition; different people call it different things. He called it wild-creature knowing, a special kind of awareness that comes from inside someplace, not made of seeing, hearing, smelling, or touching. But every wild creature had it in varying degrees. It was as necessary to staying alive in the wild country as breathing.

He moved the horse slowly. The western kingbirds darted back and forth, flashes of gray and yellow, and the horned larks chattered. The clusters of butterfly weed were a brilliant red-orange against the dark green foliage, and box elder and hackberry grew tall. The hills seemed much the same as they had throughout the day, but now he knew someone was there. He felt it again and let his gaze sweep the land once more. This was ridged and steep-sided terrain, deep cuts in the land below where he rode and more ridges above, all of it well-forested. He searched for a valley that was shallow and wide and ran from west and east, following the directions on the letter in his jacket pocket.

The letter had been waiting for him at Joe Benny's place when he'd finished breaking trail for Joe's cattle drive. A fat advance had been with it, and the brief note: "I need a new trail broken and word has it you're the very best . . . the Trailsman." The directions had made up the rest of the envelope's contents. Good money. His kind of job. He'd rested a few days in Faro's Junction with Rita Turner. It was a good few days. Rita was proof that old lovers could be friends and friends could be lovers. The few days had been made of warm flesh, open lips and open thighs, old discoveries made new again and old ecstasies reborn.

But finally he had left, crossed into the Colorado Territory and into the high hills lush with nature's richness. He'd glimpsed bear, grizzly, herds of white-tailed deer, and plenty of muskrat and beaver. He slowed the horse again as he squinted across the hilly terrain. The Pawnee rode these hills and sometimes the Arapaho came down from the north and Kiowa from the south. But he didn't feel Indian. Didn't smell them, either—the odors of fish oil and bear grease mixing in with their perspiration. There was something else, and he had gone on for some two hundred yards more when he spotted the rider below, moving slowly in a cut of land.

He stayed on the ridge and moved the pinto forward, drawing almost parallel to the rider below, and halted under the branches of a thick box elder. He peered down at a slender figure, dark brown hair cut short, a tan shirt tucked into brown riding britches. He frowned as he watched the young woman lean from the saddle as she rode, plainly searching the ground for tracks. He was about to move from beneath the branches of the box elder when he caught the sound—only a moment's click of a bit chain against the bit, but his wild-creature hearing had detected it. The sound had come from above him, and his eyes flicked to a ridge some two dozen yards higher up on the hillside. He saw the horseman at once, saw the man raising a rifle to his shoulder, the barrel directed down at the young woman below.

Skye Fargo frowned as he took a split second to measure distance. It was too far for accuracy with a handgun, and he reached down and pulled the big Sharps from its saddle holster. The girl had shifted direction slightly and the rifleman was still trying to line her up in his sights. Fargo brought the Sharps up, aiming with the instant precision that years had honed to a fine art. He had no idea what this was all about, why the rifleman was about to shoot the young woman. He didn't want killing, not without explanation, reasons, justification. But the man was about to shoot, he saw. Fargo's finger closed on the trigger of the big Sharps and the rifle barked a fraction of a second before the man fired.

Fargo saw the man's rifle leap out of his hands as the bullet smashed into his arm just above the wrist. He fell from the far side of his horse and Fargo moved forward to look down at the young woman below. She was staring up at him and he saw her yank the six-gun from the holster at her side and fire, two shots that whistled past his head. He ducked but another two shots exploded, these two coming closer, and he flung himself sideways from the saddle and hit the ground, rolled, came up on one knee.

"No. Hold it there, hold it!" he shouted, and broke off as another shot exploded. The shot had drowned out his call and he realized that she wouldn't listen if she'd heard him. She thought he'd taken the shot at her. He was the only one she'd seen. He rose to a crouch, moved forward, and peered cautiously over the edge of the ridge. He saw that the saddle was empty; she had leaped from her horse. Then two more shots echoed through the hills and sent small showers of dirt into his face. She had also reloaded. He fell backward, lay still, and cast a glance at the high ridge. The horse and the rifleman were gone, he with a bullet in his forearm. Fargo swore softly. He was left with a young woman certain he had tried to kill her. He had to try to reach her. He flattened himself on his stomach and crawled to the edge of the ridge again and peered down the slope. Nothing moved.

"Ho, down there. Listen to me," he called. "You're making a mistake. You've got it all wrong." He paused, listening and his only answer was silence. "Come out and we can talk," he said. "I'll come out, too," he tried. Again there was only silence, and he frowned as he wondered whether she had managed to sneak away. He pulled himself closer to the edge to get a better view of the bottom of the slope. The shot slammed into the dirt only an inch from his shoulder and he rolled and skittered back from the edge. "Damn," he swore aloud.

She wasn't about to believe in words and he swore again at her distrust even as he realized he couldn't blame her. Words were cheap. They all too often cloaked trickery. But he'd not stay trapped on the ridge like a rabbit by some six-gun-toting furious female. Besides, his curiosity was thoroughly aroused now. He moved back a few feet farther and let his eyes scan the ridge until he found the length of log, partly rotted on one side. He crawled to it, saw that it was some five feet in length. It would do perfectly. A line of dense brush and bur oak ran down the near side of the slope all the way to the bottom, and Fargo pulled the log closer. From the direction of the last shot, she was lying at the very edge of the line of trees and brush, her eyes on the ridge, waiting for him to show himself again.

Fargo moved a few feet farther back at the top of the tree and brush line, lifted the log, and sent it crashing down through the trees. The foliage shook violently as the log rolled and tumbled down the slope, sounding exactly as he'd wanted it to sound, as though someone were racing with wild abandon down the slope in the heavy brush and tree cover. He was smiling as the next sound erupted, a volley of gunshots, and he raced to the edge of the ridge. The shots were coming from inside a cluster of brush, following the path of the sound. If it had been someone crashing down the slope, one shot at least would've winged him.

Fargo counted off the shots, and when the sixth one resounded, he leaped down over the edge of the ridge and half slid, half ran down the slope to reach her before she could reload. She had just jammed the first cartridge into the gun when he reached her, and she whirled to bring the revolver up and fire. But he came in low with a flying tackle that caught her around the knees. She went down and the shot exploded harmlessly into the air. "Damn, little hellcat," he swore as he avoided a raking swipe of her nails and managed to close one hand around her wrist. He twisted and she gasped in fury and pain as the gun fell from her hand. She tried to raise a knee and sink it into his groin, but he felt her leg move, twisted, and she only got a piece of his outer thigh. He swore again, got his other hand on her arm, and flung her onto her back.

He was on top of her at once, holding her arms pinned against the ground. "Stop it, damn it," he rasped. Brown eyes shot fury at him out of an attractive face—a short, straight nose and even features, with lips that were no doubt nicely shaped when not biting down on each other.

"Bastard," she spat at him.

He pushed himself to his feet, yanked her up with him, and shook her as though she were a rag doll, her head snapping back and forth. "I didn't fire at you," he yelled when he stopped shaking her. "You hear me, you damn spitfire?"

She glowered back, found her breath. "Some damn squirrel did it? You were the only one up there," she said.

"No, there was someone else, on the ridge above me," Fargo said. "He had his rifle aimed for you. I shot him to stop him."

"You expect me to believe that?" she sneered.

He took his hands from her arms. "No, you couldn't do that, could you?" he tossed back.

She flung a glance up at the high ridge. "Where is this someone else? You said you shot him."

"I wounded him. He got away. That was your doing," Fargo snapped.

"My doing?"

"Yes, you had me so busy dodging bullets he got the chance to take off," Fargo accused. Her eyes narrowed, but he saw neither fear nor acceptance in them. He had to break through her wall of skepticism. "Why aren't you dead?" he flung at her, and she met his stare. "If I tried to kill you, why haven't I finished it?" he pressed.

She glowered back. "I don't know. Maybe you're still going

to. Maybe you'll take your time. Maybe you're a damn crazy,'' she said. "But I don't buy words, mister."

He grasped hold of her wrist and flung her forward. "Start climbing, dammit," he growled, and she turned and started to pull herself up the slope ahead of him. He watched her as he followed, and took in a long, slender figure, a trim, tight rear, a strong back under the tan shirt that fitted tightly, and breasts that seemed on the shallow side yet filling out at the bottoms. They moved as she climbed, swayed with the pull of her body.

He stayed with her as they reached the middle ridge and saw her quick glance at the Ovaro, her eyes pausing on the horse's jet-black fore- and hind-quarters and glistening white mid-section. "Keep going," he growled, and she continued to climb up the second slope, which turned out to be somewhat steeper than the lower one. She slipped twice, caught herself and quickly recovered. There was a lithe grace in the way her lean body moved, he noted. He finally reached the high ridge with her and stepped to the left, his gaze sweeping the ground until he found what he sought. He dropped to one knee and gestured to her, pointing out first the hoofprints still clear in the soft mountain bromegrass and then the drops of blood on the ground.

She stared down, her smooth forehead marked with a deep furrow. "I'll be damned," she muttered finally. Fargo rose to his feet to fasten her with a stern glance.

"I'd say you owe me an apology, girl," he said.

"Seems that way."

"Seems?" he pressed.

"All right, it is that way," she said with a touch of defiance.

"Apologies come hard to you, don't they?"

"I'm not used to them," she admitted.

"You've a name?"

"Names don't matter," she said. "I thank you for what you did and I'm glad I missed winging you." She turned abruptly and started down the steep slope, moving carefully, and he followed and caught up to her when she reached the ridge below, where the Ovaro waited.

"Hold on, dammit," he said, and she paused. "Why all the secrecy?"

"No secrecy. You did a good deed. I'm beholden to you for that. There's no need for anything more," she said, her expression quietly adamant.

"This whole thing's awfully strange," Fargo muttered.

"Guess so," she said.

His eyes narrowed on her. "And you still aren't sure about me, are you?"

The young woman shrugged. "Like you said, this whole thing's awfully strange, you being here at the right moment and everything."

"Luck. Good luck for you."

"Seems that way," she said.

He looked at her hard. It was becoming obvious that she wasn't about to trust in him. She was being very cautious—maybe with good reason. Maybe there were wheels within wheels. Maybe she had reason to suspect more than one enemy. "Who was the man that aimed to kill you?" he asked.

"I don't know."

"And you can't even guess," he said, sarcasm in his tone.

"I didn't say that," she returned. She paused, her brown eyes studying him for a moment longer. "Look, you seem to have done me a real favor, but you're still a stranger, mister. I don't guess with strangers."

"You don't even tell them your name," he grunted.

"Mary," she said, turned, and started down the second slope to her horse. He stayed on the ridge and watched her swing into the saddle with easy grace. "Much obliged," she called up to him with a wave, and rode into the trees.

He watched her disappear and slowly walked to the Ovaro, pulled himself into the saddle, and rode on along the ridge. It had been a strangely unsettling experience, full of things left hanging, and he always disliked that. She had been unsettling, attractive yet very walled in, almost fearful. No, that wasn't the word, he corrected himself. She had too much fight in her for that word. He cast around for another and came up with *distrust*. Monumental distrust. That fitted her better. But why? he wondered. And why had someone been out to blast her with a rifle shot? She had been surprised by the fact but not shaken and seemingly not entirely mystified.

He shook his head again. A passing incident that would likely stay unexplained. He turned his concentration back to the land as he sought the shallow valley. As he saw dusk sliding across the hills, he found a spot beneath a red cedar to camp and had the Ovaro unsaddled as night fell. The hills turned cool and he made a small fire, enough to warm some beef jerky. He stretched out his bedroll as soon as he finished eating, then undressed and lay down. He went to sleep with thoughts of the strange young woman drifting through his mind.

When he woke, the chickadees filled the morning air with their quick, three-note calls, and he found a small stream that let him wash and a wild plum arbor that let him breakfast. He rode out onto the ridge again, and followed the land as it dipped downward, high green hills staying on his right. Suddenly he caught sight of the shallow valley. He put the pinto into trot, swung into the valley, and followed it eastward, finding that it soon narrowed and became not much more than a wide path. A lake was his next landmark, and he rode into the afternoon with the high, tree-covered land still on his right.

The terrain had become less ridged and jagged now, the hills rolling more, with swooping inclines well covered with cedar, bur oak, and cottonwood. The flash of sun on blue water a few hundred yards ahead caught his eye, and he spurred the Ovaro forward along the rise of land at his right. The pleasant quiet of the day exploded with the sudden crackling sound of rifle shot, an out-of-place, obscene sound. He felt the shot cross inches in front of him and he flung himself from the saddle, hit the ground, and rolled into a low stretch of brush as another shot exploded. He had the Colt in his hand as his eyes peered at the rise of land across from him, letting his gaze move along the trees. He spied the foliage away a few dozen feet from the passageway where he'd been riding.

He watched the line of the foliage as it moved. His attacker was moving down toward level ground, and Fargo waited till the foliage swayed almost directly across from him. He raised the big Colt, wishing he'd had a chance to take the Sharps from its saddlecase, and fired two quick shots. The foliage stopped moving and he waited, watching, but nothing swayed or rustled. Was his attacker the man he'd winged on the ridge yesterday?

he wondered. It was possible. A splint on his forearm wouldn't prevent him from using a rifle. Fargo let three minutes go by and swore softly. Maybe his two shots had both landed. A stand-off wouldn't give him an answer, he knew. He had to do something to find out. He moved, rose, shook the lower branches of a young cedar, and dropped flat. Nothing happened. No rifle bullets whistled into the tree.

His eyes moved to the left, along the passageway to where it ended in a stand of red cedar, brush, and hackberry. It would give him a way to crawl to the other side and surprise someone very cagey or find someone very dead. He lay down on his stomach and began to crawl along the brush, moving slowly, almost inching his way to avoid disturbing even a leaf. He kept tossing glances across at the other side as he crawled but caught no sign of movement. The crawling was agonizingly slow, but he forced down impatience that tried to push him into moving too fast, rustling a branch or a tree. He finally reached the place where the passageway ended and he carefully turned himself, staying flat as he began to inch his way toward the other side.

He pushed high grass from in front of his face, carefully moved a piece of broken branch, and crawled forward again. He had reached the center of the trees that ended the passageway when he caught the flicker of movement in front of him. He lifted his head and found himself staring face-to-face with the figure also flattened on the ground and crawling toward him. The figure, not more than a dozen feet away, stared back, and he saw the rifle clutched in one hand. He also saw light brown hair worn loose and shoulder-length, a short, straight nose, and full cheeks and medium blue eyes that stared back at him with equal surprise.

But the moment of surprise exploded, for him and for the young woman, a simultaneous reaction. He saw her press her hand into the ground and try to bring up the rifle and he rolled, kept rolling until he came up against the wide trunk of a red cedar. He took refuge there, the Colt in hand. "What the hell is this?" he swore aloud. "Ladies Day again?"